A CLOSE SHAVE WITH THE DEVIL

For Frank

A CLOSE SHAVE WITH THE DEVIL

Stories of Dublin

★

ENA MAY

Ena May.

THE LILLIPUT PRESS
DUBLIN

First published 1998 by
THE LILLIPUT PRESS LTD
62-63 Sitric Road, Arbour Hill,
Dublin 7, Ireland.

A CIP record for this
title is available from
The British Library.

ISBN 1 901866 17 3

*The Lilliput Press receives financial assistance from
An Chomhairle Ealaíon / The Arts Council of Ireland.*

Set in 11 on 15 Bembo with display heads in Lithos Regular
Printed in Ireland by Betaprint of Clonshaugh, Dublin

CONTENTS

ITCHY RYDER
AND THE GREEN FROG

tchy Ryder lived across the road. She was the only child of Mr and Mrs Ryder and she loved frogs. You always knew when she had one on her mind or in her pocket because her eyes went all sly and dreamy. Spring was the best time for Itchy, or summer if it was wet.

Itchy was tall for her age, which was ten. She had waxy skin and sparse ginger hair which, to my Ma's amusement, her Ma called 'golden'. On account of her adenoids, she talked through her nose and it was just as well she didn't laugh a lot because when she did the smell that came out would scatter an army.

No one liked Itchy Ryder and I hated her; but she got a shilling a week pocket-money and that was sixpence more than me, so she sometimes came in handy.

Every summer gangs of us roamed Hacker's Field with jam-jars, catching bees. Itchy always came too, but never with a jar. We'd be stalking the seedy grasses and wildflowers, lids at the ready, while she crouched alone in the ditch beneath the hawthorns, poking away to her heart's content in spawny pools.

It was Mammy's opinion that Itchy's Da, Mr Ryder, was on the small side for a real man (but he was from Mullingar and she didn't like country people). He worked as a salesman in Bradley's Children's Shoe Shop in Nassau Street where you got a balloon with every pair. His skin was the colour of a Lucky Lump and his hair of old ladies' stockings. One thing about Mr Ryder was that he always used the back gate. Afraid of dirtying the hall, my Ma said out of the corner of her mouth; neither a man nor a mouse. He cycled to work along the lane by Hacker's Field, sometimes stopping to whip out binoculars because birds were his hobby. Daddy said that Wally Ryder knew more about birds than was good for him and blathered on about them in Mooney's *ad infinitum*.

Mrs Ryder was a loud-voiced, red-headed chain-smoker of Wild Woodbines, a great one for scrubbing, polishing and disinfecting all around her. Cleanliness is next to godliness she always said, smoke puffing out of her like a chimney gone on fire. Her house was so clean it smelled like a hospital and so did she; of Lifebuoy, Jeyes Fluid, mince, cigarettes and Scrubbs Ammonia.

One day I found a ball outside the tennis club and Itchy said she had lost it.

'Finders keepers,' I said, putting the ball into my pocket. 'Losers weepers.'

Itchy's eyes got slitty. She moseyed around me working up a gollier, then spat it into my face. I spat back. Howling like a cat, she grabbed one of my plaits, so I pulled her mangy scruff as hard as I could. Some came out in my hand. Then, loud enough for anyone to hear, she screamed that my Da was a drunkard, the biggest in Dublin and everyone knew. So that was that. I took her and held her under the tennis-club tap until she nearly drowned. Then I ran off, frightened.

But it served her right.

After tea that evening, Mrs Ryder came barging across shouting for my Ma, hammering on our front door. Sensing trouble, my brothers beamed, Daddy lit up the stairs to the lavatory with the *Dublin Opinion* and Mammy girded her loins by whipping off her apron and slapping on lipstick.

They met at the hall door; two mad puffed-up hens about to

peck each other to death. Neighbours gathered, shushing each other. They relaxed against railings or leaned on lawnmowers, lighting fags and sharing oranges as if they were at the pictures.

Mrs Ryder went first, Woodbine clamped in the corner of her mouth. I kept watching the ash, wondering why it didn't fall. It was longer than the fag itself and waggled up and down while she denounced me as a little brat, a scut, a savage, a brazen hussy, and a born troublemaker who shouldn't be allowed to mix with decent, respectable people.

At the word 'respectable' my Ma (it was her turn now) hooted, smirking at the audience to laugh too, which some of them did. She lifted her head in a queenly fashion and looked down the length of her nose. 'And tell us, Mrs Ryder,' she said in her best Rathmines-and-Rathgar, 'tell us as a matter of interest, how and what could *you* possibly know about respectability? And you only lately up out of a one-roomed tarmacadam shack in the depths of the Bog of bloody Allen!'

Mrs Ryder flinched. The crowd sucked in its breath. It was definitely one-nil to Mammy.

'My Astasia,' announced Mrs Ryder, recovering the power of speech, 'and her name *is* Astasia, not Itchy as you very well know. My Astasia is a delicate child and if she gets sick as a result of this vile attack, I'll be holding *you*, Mrs Doolin, personally responsible.'

Heads in the crowd nodded agreement. One-all.

'*Delicate?*' screeched Mammy, who was now in her element. 'And why wouldn't Itchy be delicate? In God's name I ask you, how could the poor unfortunate child be anything *but* delicate, God love her?' Addressing the audience. 'When we all know, the way things are, that it's a wonder she's alive at all today.'

'And what's that supposed to mean?'

'Living in an unnatural house like that—'

'Unnatural?' shrieked Mrs Ryder, scarlet, her eyes popping.

'With no healthy germs to give her protection,' said Mammy piously. Since excessive cleanliness was a Protestant trait, it was now two-one to Mammy. '*And* of course never having had a decent dinner in her life, but sure what can you expect from people who *still* drink shell cocoa even though the war is well over?'

Mrs Ryder looked baffled. You could see her mind wondering about how dinners and the war had come into it.

At that moment, as if to signal her defeat, the Woodbine ash fell onto the broad navy shelf of her bosom. She looked at me, saw me looking at it, then smashed it into a silvery smudge and walked away.

Everyone seemed to think it was a good enough row, although short. I got murdered and put to bed without any supper.

That night Daddy told Mammy that, even from the lav, she had sounded like a fishwife, and she said he was nothing but a tight-fisted yellow-belly, always was and would be till the cows came home across the sands of Dee.

A couple of times, out playing, I caught Itchy watching me with that dreamy look but I paid no attention.

Then, one morning during the holidays, she sidled up with sixpence and asked could we be friends. Being stony-broke, I said yes, but to myself 'and-no-and-maybe'. (You can do that if you cross your fingers and make sure not to be the first to speak.)

Itchy smiled her sneaky smile. 'That's great.'

The first thing in a friendship is to share your secrets, so she told me she had hair on her bum; I didn't believe it, so she pulled down her knickers in the back lane.

'It's awful,' I said, at the reddish fuzz.

'I know. I hate it.'

'So would I.'

'You get it when you're older.'

'Is it prickly?'

'No.'

'It looks it.'

'You bleed too.'

'What?'

'I read it in a book in the tallboy. Out of your bottom. Girls bleed red and boys bleed white. Every week.'

I knew she was making it up but I didn't let on.

My secret was about my Da's gun on the back of the door, from the Emergency.

'Your Da's not a soldier,' said Itchy.

'It's an LDF gun. He forgot to give it back.'

'What's LDF?'

'A kind of an army in case of Hitler.'

I didn't tell her that Mammy said the LDF was just an excuse for grown men who should have a bit more sense to go cavorting around the Dublin mountains playing Cowboys and Indians with red and blue ink in their little water-pistols.

'That might be why Hitler never came to Ireland,' Itchy said.

'It is.'

We ran down to Cully's and spent the tanner on two twopenny wafers, a pennyworth of Nancy Balls and a penny Plug Tobacco. Mr Cully's daughter, Maggie, was on her high stool trying to add it all up with a purple pencil when two boys I didn't know swaggered into the shop.

'Hey, missis,' said one, who had a big bursty boil on the side of his neck. 'Wudja give us—'

'We're first,' I said.

'Shurrup you, ya little sparrow fart, or I'll dye yer eye f'yeh.'

He winked mightily at the pal, then leaned over the counter into Maggie's face. 'Wudja ever do us a favour, pet?' he said softly.

Maggie said nothing. Her eyes were like saucers. The pal giggled and squirmed.

'How about a few jelly babies?'

'Da!' screamed Maggie.

The boys fled. Mr Cully leapt out of the back room, sweeping-brush in hand. He chased them down the road, waving the brush and shouting in bad language, but they jumped onto the back of a passing Swastika Laundry van and got clean away.

'What did they do anyway?' he asked, returning red-faced, his hair down on one side like an oily waterfall. 'Rob or what?'

Maggie, beetroot, just shrugged in a sulky fashion.

I came to the rescue. 'They only wanted jelly babies, Mr Cully.'

'Brats!' he snapped. 'That's all they are.'

He looked at himself in a 'Players Please' mirror, lifted the fallen-down hair and plastered it back over the baldy patch. 'Gurriers!'

Eamonn, the baker's horse, was outside the shop waiting for the breadman to come from the Widow's where he went every day for his oats.

'Maggie Cully's an awful eejit,' said Itchy.

I nodded. But in my heart I felt sorry for Maggie, sitting in her Da's dingy shop all day, measuring ounces of tea and sugar into screws for poor people and tying sticks into bundles for kindling.

I patted Eamonn. 'Give him a Nancy Ball, Itch, to see will he eat it.'

'I will not.'

'You have twelve.'

'I don't care. I'm not going to waste a good Nancy Ball on a horse. An' anyway, I hate horses. They're stupid. I'm going.'

I caught up with her and we went along linking arms, licking our wafers and happily swopping whoppers about the other girls on our road.

At Itchy's suggestion, we went into Hacker's Field and lay down in the grass. The air was hot, heavy with the creamy scent of the hawthorns. Except for birds, bees, grasshoppers, and the faint steady heartbeat from the mill at the end of the lane, it was as peaceful as anything.

Itchy divided the Nancy Balls. Eight for her. Four for me. I didn't mind. It was her money and, anyway, Nancy Balls weren't my favourites.

It was too hot to do anything. Except maybe go to the Baths if you had the money, but I hadn't and anyway my togs were lost. I stretched out in the sun, as content as a cat.

It got suddenly dark and cool. I opened my eyes. Itchy was standing, bending towards me, a tall black figure between me and the sun. Her face was in shadow but I knew she was staring down at me.

'What it is, Itch? What's up?'

'Nothing.'

She straightened up and ran off.

'Where are you going?'

'Nowhere. I'll be back in a minute.'

She disappeared down into her favourite place, in under the hawthorns.

Frog-hunting, I thought, wishing I had a jam-jar because the purple clover and briar-roses were alive with fat, feasting bumblers, all powdery with pollen.

I rolled over onto my belly. The grass smelled lovely, hot and green. Tiny birds flew in and out of bushes. A ladybird landed on a thick blade of grass and hurried along it. 'Ladybird, ladybird, fly away home,' I whispered. 'Your house is on fire, your children are gone. All but one and her name is Ann. And she crept under the pudding-pan.' The ladybird stopped for a moment to think about it, then spread her wings and flew away home. They always do.

From across the canal came the lonely whistle of the Cork train. The Angelus bell rang. My stomach rumbled the way it always does when it's nearly dinner-time. I decided to go after Itchy.

It was dark in the ditch, black as pitch after the sun, and as cold as my dead Grandpa's forehead when they made me kiss him. Itchy was hunkered down in the mud in front of a huge frog that was staring back at her as if she was its long-lost Granny. It was horrible; slimy and green, with big bulgy eyes and sides that plopped in and out like the soft part on the top of a new baby's head that you're not supposed to touch or it'll die.

'Uuagh!' I couldn't help shivering.

Neither it nor Itchy moved an inch.

'It's awful in here. There's an awful stink.'

Itchy whirled around in a fury. 'Shut up, you!'

'Shut up yourself! I'm going home for my dinner.'

She hurried after me, broke the Plug Tobacco on a stone and offered me the bigger half. 'Ah, don't go, Eily. Please.'

'Well … okay.'

We wet the last Nancy Ball and rubbed it on for lipstick. Then Itchy made a roundy mark in the middle of our foreheads.

'The secret mark,' she laughed.

I moved away on account of her smell and suddenly didn't want to be on my own with her any longer. 'Come on, we'll go and play skipping.'

'Ah, it's too hot for skipping.'

She was right there.

'There's this game we play down the country,' she said slowly.

'What game?'

'It's massive.'

'How d'you play it?'

'Cinchy. One's a policeman and the other's captured and the policeman comes along and … look, I'll tell you what, we'll play it and I'll explain as we're going along.'

'Alright.'

'I'll be the policeman and … gimme your belt.'

She bound my hands behind my back with the belt of my frock, then lay me down and tied my feet together with the laces from my runners.

'It's too tight.'

'It'll loosen up.'

'My blood will stop.'

'No, it won't.'

'It's hurting, Itchy.'

'Quit complaining.'

'It's miles too tight.'

She shoved my hankie into my mouth. It went so far down my throat that I nearly choked. I retched and grunted, pleading with my eyes.

'You have to have it, so's no one can hear.' She stood up, looked down at me and smiled her awful smile. 'You're like a stuffed chicken, all trussed up and ready for the oven.'

I could've brained her.

'Now, I'm the policeman on the beat and I come along and find you. Close your eyes.'

I closed them. I would've done anything she asked. The hankie was drying up my spit and the laces biting like wire into my ankles.

'Moan!' Her voice came from a distance. 'And keep your eyes closed.'

I moaned.

'Act louder, so's the policeman can hear you.'

I did, but it wasn't acting. I felt awful and already hated this game as much as I hated Itchy Ryder.

The next thing I knew she was crouched over me. 'I'll teach you to nearly drown me,' she hissed, pushing the green frog towards my face. 'See it? See? He's looking for his mark. His secret mark. The mark of the frog. You're a frog lover now, Eily Doolin, ha-ha-ha!'

She screeched with laughter, pulled up my frock, opened the waistband of my knickers and flung the frog inside.

I froze, rigid with fear; went blind, deaf and dumb all in an instant. I think I died for a while. Then, as through a haze, I saw Itchy dancing around me, cackling like a Hallowe'en witch. Then she was gone. And there was silence.

And I was alone.

Alone with the frog.

Which soon tried to free itself but couldn't on account of the strong elastic in my school knickers. I tried screaming, but thanks to the hankie, even Superman's X-ray ears couldn't have heard the squeaks that came out of me.

Then, through the bushes, I saw Mr Ryder cycling up the lane for his dinner. Dear Jesus, let him look at birds, I prayed. Please please, dear Jesus, let him! He passed by just as if I wasn't lying there dying in a field.

Jesus had forsaken me!

I gave up and fainted and when I came to, the first thing I saw was a rock with sharp edges in a clump of nettles.

If I got over to it and rubbed my belt against it, like they do in the pictures, I'd be free. Using my elbows and feet to propel myself, I inched like a reluctant crab towards my destination.

I distinctly felt each of the first three stings: one on my right arm under my elbow, the next along the side of my right leg, the third on the back of it. Then it seemed that my entire body was on fire; my arms, legs and back, even my head and ears were aflame with pain. I heard myself moaning and crying, but in the distance. At last I got to the rock. I propped myself against it, and kept rubbing and rubbing until the belt broke and my hands were free. I pulled the hankie up out of my red, raw throat and got sick all over myself.

Then, holding my breath and trying not to think about it, I opened the waistband of my knickers.

It was sitting there on my vest, fat, green and shiny, so still and calm that it could've been made out of Connemara marble, and so much at home it seemed a shame to disturb it.

'Waugh!' I shouted, in as fierce a voice as I could manage. 'Waugh!'

It didn't move a muscle; just gazed back at me as though in polite enquiry. In the end I had to hoosh it away with a stick.

I ran all the way home crying, sticky with tears, snot and vomit, my wrists and ankles chafed and bleeding. 'In the wars again, Eily?' someone asked.

Mammy had no sympathy; I should know better than to go into Hacker's or *anywhere* with that little brat Itchy Ryder; it was my own fault and anyway, I should fight my own battles and not come running to her. But later, after bathing my wrists and ankles and bandaging them in clean hankies, she said that if it was any consolation, the poor frog was probably more frightened than I was.

It wasn't any consolation.

I had nightmares: green frogs by the hundred in my bedroom, on the walls, the ceiling, the wardrobe, the eiderdown, my pillow. I'd run to get away but they'd be under my feet, squelching, and I'd tumble, trying to scream, down into them.

Knowing the nightmares wouldn't stop until I paid Itchy back, I decided to get her with the gun on the back of the door for the Emergency; but it was no use because, although I searched every hidey-hole in the house for ages, I never managed to find any ammo.

Then it said in the *Evening Mail* that Saint Martin de Porres never refuses a request, so I requested an idea. And what should I see the very next Saturday coming home from the pictures only Mr Ryder's bike waiting against the wall of Mooney's pub. It wasn't exactly Itchy but it was better than nothing so I bent down and let the air out of *both* the tyres.

Well, it served them right.

The nightmares went away immediately; but catching bees in Hacker's Field was never the same.

THE RED SANDALS

W e hadn't got a car but at the bottom of our back garden we had a garage with a sloping asbestos roof that soaked up the sun, a good place to lie when you wanted to read in peace or eat sweets without having to share. The only snag was that, after a while, the ridges stuck into your back.

One sunny morning I was lying there with a French Nougat when Mr Smith's head popped like a prairie-dog through the roof-window of his workshop.

'Lovely morning.'

'Yes.'

'No school today?'

'No, we got our holidays.'

'Lucky you.'

Even though he was only three doors up, I didn't know Mr Smith very well because he was from England and hadn't been living in Blarney Park for very long. He wore cravats and was my Ma's idea of a proper English gentleman, although downtrodden, God love him, and way too small.

'Well then, back to work.'

He gulped in air, waved goodbye and disappeared.

Except for a dwarf once in the Whitehall carnival, Mr Smith was the smallest man I had ever seen. His wife was the biggest woman: as broad as a Guinness barge, hefty as a whale; so big that you felt sorry for her bike when she sat on it, the sad squish of the tyres, and the squeak of the saddle when her big roundy bottom enfolded it. She looked down at you from her great height as though you were an ant she might squash with her sensible brogues. Instead of talking in an ordinary voice, she boomed in an Englishy accent, as if she thought you were deaf or miles up a hill and she was down it.

Mammy said Mrs Smith was a perfect lady, a model for all, whose manners and general deportment suggested an upper-class, superior type who had once come out of the top drawer.

It must've been huge.

At Mass one Sunday morning I saw her being holier than anyone in the front row.

'I thought all English were Protestants,' I said on the way home.

'No,' said Mammy. 'Not *all*. You'll find the odd Catholic there alright, but just the odd one. But they're not *real* Catholics, if you know what I mean. Not as real as us.'

Once, in the course of lecturing me and Patrick in the middle of the road about the virtues of cabbage, Mrs Smith asked what we'd had for our dinner. 'Peas and bones!' shouted Patrick, who was going on six. She laughed like a hippopotamus on a bike and cycled off. Mammy flew into a rage when I told her. 'Bones? I'll give you bones,' she shrieked, running after Patrick, flicking wet tea-towels. 'Chops if you don't mind. Bloody lamb chops.'

Mrs Smith kept herself busy performing good deeds and corporal works of mercy (usually involving cabbage) on the deserving poor of her adopted city. It was one way of ensuring a good place in heaven. As ye sow, so also shall ye reap, she'd bawl from her bike, her face red with righteousness. The hungry sheep look up and are not fed!

On account of its healthful properties, Mrs Smith grew nothing but cabbage in her back garden. She ate mounds of it daily, bottling the water for use as (a) a kidney-flushing drink, (b) a hair-tonic, to revitalise the scalp and discourage nits, (c) a foot-bath, to harden the soles. When she sat out in the back garden on a summer's evening with her feet in a basin of steamy cabbage water, you could smell it a mile off with a peg on your nose. Daddy said the pong would weaken the hardest man's stomach, let alone a little pipsqueak like *him* (meaning Mr Smith).

Every Saturday morning Mrs Smith trundled off on her bike under an emerald mountain of curly Savoy destined for the destitute of Dublin.

The Smiths had one grown-up son, James Edward, who lived in South Africa, where he owned a goldmine. Mrs Smith proclaimed that she wasn't one to boast, but she never lost an opportunity to talk about dear James; how clever he was, how handsome, and how remarkable were his achievements.

As if anyone else gave a damn.

Dear James was the one thing about Mrs Smith that gave Mammy a pain in the face, though she'd have died rather than admit it.

Mrs Smith once went on a visit to James in South Africa, and when she came back Mammy invited her in for an afternoon tea of cucumber sandwiches with the crusts cut off and butterfly-buns. Her face was red and brown. It had been unbearably hot, she said, and droned on and on about dear James, his superb home and standard of living, until I fell asleep. When I woke up, she was giving out about the natives; how each man, woman and child was a lazy, lying savage who performed their natural functions in the bush and who, if you put a Hoover into their hands, stood gawking at it, giggling, with their legs wide apart.

Mammy tut-tutted. 'Go 'way. Imagine that. Goodness gracious. A bun, Mrs Smith?'

The great jaws opened like a slow-motion crocodile and a whole butterfly-bun disappeared, leaving only a stripe of jammy cream on her upper lip.

'Mammy?'

'What?'

'What's a natural function?'

'Nothing. Keep quiet. Children should be seen and not heard. Another cup, Mrs Smith?'

Mrs Smith removed the remains of the butterfly-bun with a hankie that looked like a penny stamp in her huge hands. 'Oh yes indeed, Mrs Doolin, we have much to be thankful for.' She held out her cup and fixed me with a look. 'You should be thankful, Eily, every moment, for all you have. Thankful that you're a good Catholic child and not a little black savage running around the jungle all day with nothing on.'

I nodded with my holy face on, but would've given anything to be a savage running around a jungle with nothing on.

'I hope you put your weekly penny in the black-baby box in school?'

'Yes, Mrs Smith,' I said sweetly, knowing that my black-baby money usually went on a Plug Tobacco, Lucky Lump or a Giftie Bar.

'Conversion is their only hope, you understand,' said Mrs Smith, as another whole butterfly vanished into the maw.

On my way home from tap-dancing the following Saturday, I saw a tall, shiny black man with books under his arm strolling out through the gates of Trinity College. In flowing, coloured robes and with his head wrapped in cloths of gold and silver, he looked more like a king than a savage; but he was black, so he must have been.

I was in no hurry, so in case he was heading for the bushes in Stephen's Green to perform his natural function, I decided to tail him. Halfway up Grafton Street he met another tall black man and, talking and laughing just like ordinary people, but black and with whiter teeth, they went into Bewley's Oriental Café.

I stood there, disappointed, watching the man roasting coffee-beans in the window, sniffing the lovely brown smell.

My older brother Andy roared laughing in bed that night. He said that I was an awful eejit because performing a natural function was only going to the lav. I was disgusted; I had been thinking it was torturing or drinking babies' blood or sticking pins in voodoo dolls or interesting things like that.

★

I was reading a comic on the roof one Saturday morning and admiring my beautiful new red sandals when Mr Smith hailed me.

'Hello. What're you reading?'

'*The Radio Fun.*'

'Arthur Askey in it?'

'Yes.'

'"ello playmates!'

His accent was funny. He started to sing.

> *Big-hearted Arthur that's me,*
> *Clean if I'm not very clever,*
> *But only cos I want to be.*

We laughed. His eyes twinkled, crinkling at the sides.

'Enjoying your holidays?'

'Yes, thanks.'

It was a lovely morning. The sky was as blue as a Reckitt's blue-bag and under it birds flew around, chasing each other. The only thing was I had a blister on my heel and I wished I had something to eat.

'I'm making a cup of tea now,' said Mr Smith.

I sat up in spite of the ridges. 'Tea?'

'Yes. Like a cup?'

'Have you got any biscuits?'

'Biscuits.'

'I don't like tea much all by itself. I need biscuits to swallow it,' I explained.

'Oh.'

'Any kind, except arrowroot. I don't like them.'

'I see.'

'Or I wouldn't mind a bun or cake or even bread and butter if there's nothing else.'

He looked doubtful. 'Well, I don't know. There might be some biscuits in the house. I'll have a look. Just a moment.' His head disappeared.

I waited hopefully. One good thing about people with no children in the house is that they usually have biscuits. The thought made my mouth water. I was suddenly starving for biscuits.

The next minute his head shot through the roof. 'You're in luck, Eily.'

'What kind?'

'Well, I don't know. They seem to be marshmallow. Pink and white. With coconut on.'

'Coconut creams!'

'Is that so?'

'My third favourites.'

I climbed down into the back lane, being careful not to scrape my sandals off the wall.

Mr Smith opened a small door in the big garage-door of his workshop. It was like stepping into the Snow Queen's palace. Everything icy white. The floor, walls, cupboards, ceiling, all the surfaces and shelves. Sparkling mouthfuls of teeth gaped from glass jars. A white-painted ladder led up to the open roof-window. Another window in the back wall looked into the garden where rows of cabbages stood like stiff green sentries.

I looked at the teeth. 'You make them, don't you?'

He nodded sadly. 'I do.'

'Do you not *like* making them?'

'Not particularly.'

'Why not?'

'I don't get any satisfaction from it.'

'Why not?'

'It's a lonely occupation.'

'Why do you do it?'

He shrugged. 'I simply fell into it.'

'Why is it lonely? Do you not see the people?'

'Who?'

'The people you make the teeth for.'

'No. The dentist does that; lets me know what needs doing. And I do it. That's all there is to it.'

He washed his hands at a stone sink and dried them in a white roller-towel hanging on the back of the door.

'Say you saw someone you didn't know laughing with false teeth walking down the road, would you know if they were yours?'

He thought for a moment. 'If there was something remarkable about them, something that had needed special attention, I suppose I would, yes. Perhaps.'

'I'd love to be able to make teeth.'

He gave a big sigh as if to say he didn't think so.

'It'd be very *handy*,' I insisted.

'It's a useful skill alright. I *suppose*,' he added, sounding rather dreary.

He was a nice-looking little man when you saw him up close. His skin had the biscuity sheen of a very dear French doll I had seen once in Pim's toy department, the kind of skin it's nice to touch. He had soft grey eyes and, except for some hay-coloured fluff around the edge of his head, was as bald as an egg.

He poured tea into two china cups and offered me a biscuit, apologising for the fact that there were only three.

'I don't bother with biscuits myself.'

'Coconut creams are my next favourites after Kimberley and USA,' I told him.

'Good.'

'Do you make your own?'

'My own. Biscuits?'

'No. Teeth.'

We laughed at the joke.

'Oh, no, Eily, no. Mine are my own, I'm happy to say. Still my own. Every one.'

'They're lovely and white like a film star's. Do you use Gordon Moore's Cosmetic Toothpaste?'

He laughed again.

So I laughed too, although I didn't know at what, and took another biscuit. I looked out the window into the garden. 'I bet you like cabbage,' I said.

His face twinged as if with a sudden toothache. He held up his hand. 'If you please, Eily. No mention of that in my domain.'

'Of cabbage?'

He shuddered. 'Noxious stuff.'

'What's noxious?'

'Awful.'

'Yeah. I hate cabbage too. But not as much as Brussels sprouts.' We drank our tea in silence for a moment. 'What's a domain, Mr Smith?'

'A domain is ...' He looked around. 'A world. My domain is my sphere, my dominion, my life. What little life I have. Am allowed.'

Through the roof-window came the song of a blackbird and of Hippo-Joe in the tennis club whistling as he cut the grass.

'New sandals, Eily?'

'Yes.'

'They're lovely.'

'I only got them the other day.'

'A pretty colour.'

'They were fifteen-and-eleven. I got a balloon with them too, in Bradley's, that the conductor burst in the bus coming home but he couldn't help it cos it was full.'

'That's a shame.'

'The only thing is they're too big. Mammy always gets things too big for growing into but sometimes by that time they're nearly worn out and I have a blister on my heel. I always get them from new shoes.'

'Oh dear, dear.' He was all concern. 'Have you a plaster on it?'

'No. We hadn't got any.'

Without further ado, he removed a dinky First-Aid box from a cupboard, knelt down, removed my sandal and, holding my foot in both hands, examined the blister.

'Oh-oh, that looks nasty.' He blew to cool it and then pressed an Elastoplast over it without hurting. 'The other?'

'No, it's fine, thanks.'

'Best to harden the foot up, I think.'

Humming to himself, he filled an enamel basin with warm water, took the towel off the back of the roller, opened a bar of Yardley's Lavender soap and lathered it up.

'Lovely slender little foot,' he murmured, lowering my good foot into the water.

'The man in Bradley's said I had *big* feet for my age. Very big.'

'Big feet so,' he smiled. 'Lovely slim *big* feet.'

He dried my foot carefully, then rubbed sweet-smelling lotion in, making me squirm and giggle.

'It tickles.'

'It might be a good idea to rest the sandals for a day or two, to give the blister a chance to heal.'

'But I've only my school shoes and they're too heavy and black, and anyway I hate them.'

'I know what you mean.' He indicated his own clumpy boots. 'How would you like to have to wear these all the time?'

I didn't want to hurt his feelings, so I just shrugged.

'No. And neither do I. But I have no choice. They're bought *for* me. Built to last, to give good service. Unlike me,' he smiled sadly. 'My feet are small, Eily. Like the rest of me. Slightly built. I'm lost in these…' He looked around the workshop. 'In these …'

'Canal-barges?' I suggested.

He looked surprised.

'That's what my Ma calls big shoes.'

'How appropriate. Except there's something rather lovely about a barge going along a canal, don't you think?' He smiled and picked up my sandals. 'They're pretty aren't they? And so soft. Soft as glove leather.'

'They still gave me a blister.'

'I'd love to, eh … could I try them on?'

'You?'

'Yes. May I?'

'If you like, but they won't fit.'

'I have small feet, Eily,' he said, starting to remove his boots and thick hairy socks. 'Very small. For my age.'

He had, too: milky baby feet, with toes curling under like little pink snails.

I laughed. 'They're smaller than mine.'

He was delighted to hear it.

After putting on my sandals, he rolled up the turn-ups of his trousers to see better. His ankles were as delicate as a chicken's. Up and down he strolled, testing, like you do in a shop, to get the feel. Then suddenly, he whooped and gave a hop, skip and jump for joy.

'They suit you, Mr Smith. They do. Even though you're a man.'

'But only a small one, Eily. A very small one.'

He laughed like a boy and took my hands and we danced around his white workshop together, laughing, singing, twirling and whirling, until we seemed to be the centre of a silver spinning crystal.

Suddenly we stopped. 'Christ Jesus,' he said softly, dropping my hands.

He was looking behind him, like Lot's wife, to where Mrs Smith stood at the workshop window, huff-puffing on the glass.

'That's it,' Mr Smith said sadly. 'That's the end of it.'

Before I could ask of what, the door opened and Mrs Smith crashed through, her face the same colour as her bright purple frock. 'And what's the meaning of this?' she bellowed, as if she had caught us doing something wrong.

Mr Smith said nothing. Just shook his head, sat on the floor and began to take off my sandals.

'Well?' shouted Mrs Smith. 'Up to your old tricks again, eh? You and your bloody … feet!'

'We were dancing, Mrs Smith,' I said.

'Hah!'

After a look that nearly cut me in half, she rushed towards Mr Smith as if to kick him into the middle of next week. Then she stopped and stood right over him, breathing down so ferociously that his wispy hair blew like straws in the wind.

His eyes were frightened. He looked like a little grey monkey at the bottom of a purple mountain.

'I'd better go,' I said. 'My dinner'll be ready. Irish stew today. Bye-bye. Thanks very much, Mr Smith, for doing my foot.'

He groaned as if a knife had been stuck into his heart.

Mrs Smith held the door open. I stepped through it into the back lane. Before I could get away, her hand gripped my shoulder and she leaned down towards me. I got her strong cabbagey smell. She made a scissors of her fingers, stuck out her tongue and pretended to cut it off. 'That's what happens to little girls who tell tales,' she whispered.

I lay on the roof until my Ma shouted 'Dinner'. But then, remembering my comic, I shinned down the wall, went back to the workshop and knocked on the door. No answer. But I knew there was someone there because I could hear a noise, a quiet, slow creak, like the tick of an old clock in a country kitchen. In case of Mrs Smith, I didn't knock again but found a crack in a knothole and looked through.

Mr Smith was swinging gently from a rafter on the end of a thick rope. His face was purple. His tongue was sticking out.

Directly opposite me, looking in from her garden of cabbages, was Mrs Smith—smiling like a crocodile that had swallowed Tarzan.

As soon as the fuss was over, she went off to live in South Africa with dear James.

A SUNDAY VISIT

W e were the only people on the road with a maid, except for the Brocks but you wouldn't mind them. Her name was Kathleen Farrell and she came from Mayo. Mammy got her in a Home that was run by nuns for girls who had got into trouble, I don't know what, but it could have been to do with babies; it usually is, when the women bend their heads together like that and talk in whispers, nodding, like birds on the edge of a lake.

Kathleen said the nuns were good to her. Saints, she said they were.

She had a room all to herself in our house, the box-room, with new pink-flowered wallpaper and a white distempered ceiling. Daddy made a dressing-table for her out of two orange-boxes held together by planks at the back, with a space for your legs. Mammy lined it with left-over wallpaper and skirted it in rose-pink taffeta. It was beautiful; as good as one you'd see in a shop any day of the week. There was a cherry-pink silken bedspread, a brown wardrobe with a handle that sometimes came off in your hand, a picture of Our Lady, and the bockety blue chair with the straw bottom.

'What's *that* doing there?' asked my Ma, about the chair.

'Nothing,' said Daddy.

'There's no need for a chair in a bedroom.'

'But—'

'Bedrooms are for *sleeping*. Not sitting in.'

'I know, love, but do you not think—'

'*No.*'

Daddy threw his eyes up to heaven, started singing 'Swanee River' and took the chair downstairs.

'It's lovely, isn't it, Mammy?' I said, inhaling the smell of fresh distemper.

'Hm! Too good for the likes of her.'

Mammy thought all country people were sleeveens who should stay down in the bogs where they belonged and not be coming up to Dublin to take the jobs. She probably forgot that Daddy was from the country because it was ages ago and he hardly ever went back, even though my Cork Granny with the whiskers was still alive.

I liked what country people I knew, like Da's relations, although when Mammy was around, I didn't pretend to: the women, with their accents, their cheerful, red cheeks and brown eggs in baskets, and the brawny, quiet, Fruito-sucking men, up for the matches in Croke Park on Sundays.

The day Kathleen arrived with her brown suitcase, Mammy was at the clinic with Andy's flat feet, so me and Daddy brought her up to the room.

'Tis beautiful,' she whispered.

Daddy beamed, pleased as Punch.

'Too good for the likes of me,' Kathleen said.

'Not at all, not a bit of it. Well, I'll leave you to get settled in so.'

I stayed to help her unpack and see what she had in the case. It wasn't much: a thick brown skirt, two white blouses, a vest with flowers on it, a piece of red flannel, a blue nightdress, a daily Missal, a post-office savings book, a bar of Knight's Castile, a box of Bourjois rouge, and a yellowing photograph of an old house with blurry people leaning against it.

'Is that your house?'

She sighed. 'It is. My old home.'

'Where is it?'

'Claremorris. Well, near enough to.'

I didn't know where that was, so I said nothing.

'In Mayo,' she said, reading my thoughts. 'The county of Mayo.'

I nodded.

'And do you know where that is?'

'Down the country.'

'It is. In the west. Do you know which side the west is on?'

'We don't learn that until fifth and I'm only in fourth.'

'I see. Well, I'll show you now and then you'll know before you start.' She made a small pink mound in the bedspread. 'This is Ireland. And here we are in Dublin, on the east, the right-hand side, the side you bless yourself with,' pointing a finger that was as skinny and quavery as a spider's leg. 'Over here on the left, you have the west, d'you see that now? The north, and the west.'

I did see it and never forgot it.

'Are you from a farm?'

'Aye, we did have a farm. Once …'

She began to unfold her clothes onto the bed.

'What animals?'

'The usual.'

'Pigs?'

'Aye.'

'I love pigs.'

'You don't.'

'Yes, I do. I saw them at the zoo with my Granny in Children's Corner. Pink, all falling and climbing over one another. Only babies. I fed them. They're gas.'

'They're not such gas when they grow I can tell you.'

'How do you mean?'

'With their screaming.'

'Screaming?'

'Aye. On the way to the slaughtering.'

'I didn't know pigs could scream.'

'Indeed'n they can. As loud as you would yourself. And a scream that, once heard, you'd never forget. You'd think it was they *knew* their destiny, God help them.'

'How would a pig know?'

'Don't ask me but they do. They have feelings, I suppose, and are not nearly as thick as they're made out to be.'

'Any other animals?'

'A few cows, hens, and did I say geese?' She looked out the window at the houses opposite and sighed. 'Aye, a few geese. Down below in the far pond.'

'Bulls?'

'No, God love you. But a dog.'

'A dog? I love dogs. What kind of a dog?'

'Yerra, just a dog.'

'What colour?'

'Shep, he was called.'

'Shep. A sheep-dog?'

She shrugged. 'Perhaps.'

'Like Lassie?'

'Who?'

'Lassie! You know. In *Lassie Come Home*. Didja see that? It was great.'

'I didn't.'

'You should've. Didja see *The Red Shoes*?'

'No.'

'About a ballet dancer who jumps under a train at the end. It was rare. *The Wizard of Oz*?'

'I was never at the pictures.'

'*What!*'

'No.'

'Why not?'

'I just never went is all.'

I was mystified; as soon as I was able to sit up straight by myself, I'd been packed off to the pictures, like everyone else, on Saturday afternoons.

'Do they not *have* the pictures down the country?'

'They have of course,' she said indignantly. 'Haven't they The New Electric Star over beyond in Claremorris? Oh, they have them alright, never fear. I just never went is all. Too busy with the farm and all.'

'Well, if you brought me to the farm sometime, on your day off maybe, I could bring you to the pictures.'

'But I couldn't, alannah. Isn't that what I'm telling you? The old place is gone now.'

'Gone?'

'Aye.'

'Gone where?'

'With the wind. Lock, stock and barrel.'

'But ...'

'We lost it. My father ...' She stopped. Her brow furrowed, face flushed. She took a deep breath. 'He died. And my brothers, drinkers all, not a damn bit of use to anyone. And my ... my mother ... oh, things fell apart ...'

'That's a lovely vest,' I said loudly to stop her from crying, wondering why anyone in their right mind would want to embroider red and green flowers across the front of their vest.

'Mayo's colours,' she said, stroking the vest with great tenderness.

'Did you do it?'

'Aye, the embroidery. They taught me in the Home. Great needlewomen, the nuns.'

It was her lucky vest, she said. She wore it for luck, whenever Mayo played in the All-Ireland Hurling or Football Final because she loved Mayo and always would, although there was nothing and no one left for her there any longer.

The wardrobe handle came off, so I showed her the knack and took a good gander at her while she put her things away. She was tall and bony, with brown, frizzy hair and the long knobbly legs of a racehorse. Her face was bony too but not like a horse's—nicer, with milky skin and some freckles. It lit up when she smiled and made you smile too, even if you didn't feel like it. The thing was her gunner eyes, which weren't noticeable at first because she kept them cast down, as if through shyness, or there being something interesting on the floor. But then she'd look up and you'd see with a shock that each eye was trying to look in at the other and was so far in that you could hardly make out the colour, cornflower blue.

Later, she told me they all had the eyes, they were a family weakness, and that the only ones who could straighten them out were the Yanks. Kathleen believed in the Yanks the way I believed in God. They could do anything. 'Born soldiers!' she said. 'Sure didn't they win the war for us?' Hearing Frank Sinatra on the wireless: 'Listen to that. Born singers.' And once, reading a Superman comic over my shoulder: 'See what I mean, Eily? That's the Yanks for you!'

She ate her meals by herself in the cold, cramped kitchen.

'Why does Kathleen have to eat in the kitchen?' I asked one day.

'Because,' said my Ma.

'Because what?'

'Because. Just because. Because I say so.'

'But—'

'Because she's a maid and the kitchen's her place. Now stop asking questions when you don't know the answers and leave me alone.'

Kathleen got up early and went to bed late. In between she cleaned, cooked, polished, scrubbed, washed, ironed, darned, black-leaded, Brassoed, wiped faces and bottoms, fine-combed lousy heads, told stories, sang songs, peeled spuds in icy water, with no word of complaint, despite her chilblains, and kept us all quiet when Mammy had headaches. Her pay was a pound a week, all found, with Wednesday nights and every Sunday afternoon and evening off. Mammy said she had landed on the pig's back but was too bloody thick to appreciate it.

I used to look at Kathleen and wonder what kind of trouble had made her end up in a Home. It couldn't have been murder, like old man Hickey's son, or she'd be in jail for life. She couldn't have robbed a bank or jewels because then she'd be rich and not a maid. Sometimes she'd see me wondering and smile. If Mammy wasn't there, I'd smile back.

Kathleen may have been skinny but she was strong too, as strong as a horse, and soon had the house spotless and smelling of lavender, the kitchen tiles glowing Cardinal Red and the fire-grate Zebraed to silvery-blackness. She was gentle too; there was no one like her to unstick glued-up eyes, coax a splinter from a festering finger or apply a scalding bread-poultice. We all ran to Kathleen with our troubles and she never failed us. Even D.J., the baby, always bawling blue from wind, responded to Kathleen when she cradled him in her arms, singing 'Red River Valley', caressing his silky head. By the time she was halfway through, he'd be gurgling at his toes, or fast asleep blowing bubbles through his chubby cherub lips.

D.J. cried after she left us (he wasn't the only one) and wouldn't be pacified. His little heart seemed broken. Mammy said it was all her fault; she knew nothing about kids and had him spoiled, but what more could you expect from an ignorant farmer's daughter?

Kathleen didn't spend money on cigarettes or small ports and perms, like the other women, because she was saving up. She put Miner's Tan on her legs instead of stockings and didn't mind when it came off in the rain. Once, on her birthday, as a present to herself, she bought a small bottle of Californian Poppy perfume in Woolworth's in Henry Street. Every month she bought a *True Life Romance* and made it last and a half-pound of Lemon's 'Romance' or Clarnico Murray's 'Bridesmaid's Caramels', a few of which were always kept at the bottom of her bag, for emergencies. That wasn't the same emergency as the War, just cuts and stings or scraps with bullies that made you cry.

One day, seeing her remove the black knicker-elastic band from around her post-office savings book, I asked what she was saving up for.

The band snapped back. 'Nothing.' Her eyes shifted. 'Nothing at all. I'm just saving up. It's like going for a walk. You're going nowhere in particular. Just for a walk. D'you have me now?'

I did. But there was something about that foxy look that made me wonder.

Sometimes, on her Wednesday afternoons, Kathleen would collect me from school and we'd go on jaunts in the bus; to Knocksedan, where she showed me bluebells, harebells, rambling roses, cowslips, wild thyme, garlic and musk mallow; to Lucan, where we walked by the Strawberry Beds and had tea and iced fancies in a sunny café in Chapelizod, watching young men in sparkling vests row up and down the Liffey. In the autumn we collected conkers in the Finglas Woods and tumbled, laughing, among the leaves.

I never thought that Kathleen would ever leave us.

One frosty morning she was on her knees shovelling yesterday's ashes and we were having our breakfast when my brother Andy raced in waving a thin blue envelope.

'From America!' he shouted. 'A letter from America.'

We dropped our spoons in astonishment.

'Give it here,' said Mammy, red with excitement.

'It's for Kathleen,' said Andy.

Mammy clicked in annoyance and grabbed for her Gold Flake.

The rest of us watched as Kathleen, with hardly a glance at it, shoved the envelope deep into the front of her apron and got on with her shovelling.

Mammy coughed, straightened her back and put down the teapot deliberately. 'A-mer-ica.'

We all knew that tone of voice.

'I didn't know you knew anyone in *America*,' she continued to Kathleen's back.

Kathleen stopped shovelling, leaned back on her heels. 'It's just a cousin, Ma'am.'

'A *cousin*?' screeched Mammy, as if a cousin was a crime. '*I* wasn't told anything about any cousin.'

'No, well, it's just a … a second cousin. Mal.'

'*Mal*? And what's that supposed to signify? *I* was never told about any *Mal*. I was never told you *had* a cousin. Let alone *a cousin in America*.'

We all held our breath. All eyes were on Kathleen. Except for the smoke coming out of Mammy's nostrils, nothing moved. Then Kathleen put down the shovel, reached for an old newspaper and began to scrunch it up. The sound was loud in the room.

Mammy could wait no longer. 'Well?' she barked.

Kathleen stopped scrunching, to look around at Mammy. 'He used to write. Now and then. He's my uncle's … my father's brother's son. Mal. Born over there. I never met him or laid eyes on him at all.'

'And what *part* of America is he in?'

''Tis Philadelphia, Ma'am.'

'Hm!'

That seemed to be the end of it.

'Hey, give us the stamp, Kathleen, willya?' said Andy, as Kathleen criss-crossed kindling over the paper.

'Oh, let her get on with it,' snapped Mammy, giving Andy a clip on the ear. 'Before we all *freeze* to death.'

★

One Saturday afternoon, Kathleen, in one of Mammy's cast-off hats with a bunch of cherries on the brim, came to The Grand with me, Andy and Patrick. In the queue that went halfway around the block, she was as bad as any of us, pushing and shoving for no reason and shouting 'We're moving!' when we started to move. When Mighty Mouse, the commissionaire, appeared at the doors in majestic purple to single out troublemakers, Kathleen fell silent with awe. Once inside, she gazed in open admiration at the plummy, gold-trimmed usherettes and gasped, astonished, at the Grecian urns, cupids, grapes and half-naked ladies holding yards of material that were plastered all over the walls and ceilings.

'Jesus,' she groaned. ''Tis magnificent.'

Gloria, the chief usherette, added to the air of excitement and glamour by parading up and down the aisle, flicking her hips at the big boys and her torch at the brats in the woodeners.

'Give 'em a shkelp with it,' shouted Kathleen, carried away by the noise and the strong smell of piss.

The minute the clock said three the lights began to sneak down very slowly and it got a bit quieter as everyone wondered were they *really* going down? Then, at exactly the same moment, everyone *knew* they were and the roar that went up nearly drowned you.

'Hey, missus!' voices urged from behind. 'Get ridda the po.'

When I explained to Kathleen, she removed the hat without protest.

The big picture was called *The Yearling*. It was about a boy and a deer that his Da has to shoot. It was very sad. I was crying, but I wasn't the only one. You could hear sniffling all over the place. Kathleen didn't cry. She sat staring at the screen with her mouth open and shoulders hunched forward. It was as though she was in another world. The second feature was a cowboy with John Wayne and every time someone got shot, Kathleen jumped. 'Oh, Jay!' she'd gasp. 'Oh, holy divine!'

That evening, she was clearing the table when Daddy asked if she'd enjoyed the picture.

'Well, I did and I didn't. I liked the good bits well enough but not the others.'

'How do you mean?'

'Well, he shouldn't have shot that deer for a start, the poor dumb animal doing no harm to nobody.'

Mammy laughed.

Daddy frowned. 'But it doesn't *happen*, Kathleen. It's a picture.'

'Dead as a doornail, God help it.'

'But it's acting, Kathleen. Only acting. It doesn't *happen*.'

Kathleen glowered at him. 'That's what they'd have us believe, alright.'

'But it is, Kathleen. Acting. Honest to God.'

Kathleen walked to the door with her loaded tray.

'Get sense,' muttered Mammy to Daddy.

At the door Kathleen turned and addressed herself to Daddy. 'Well so, Mr D., and if it is *play-acting* as you call it, would you mind telling me what it was had the whole picture-house'—pointing at me—'herself included, destroying themselves with the crying when it got put out of its misery?'

That was Kathleen's trouble, taking things too seriously. She hated baddies, especially Edward G. Robinson. 'It wasn't the drink,' after *Key Largo*. 'God knows that young one had enough in. No. It's forcing someone to sing when they don't want to; there's nothing worse.'

Another thing she had a bee in her bonnet about was kissing. 'How would you like to be at it and have gangs gawking up at you? Let me tell you you wouldn't, and if you did there'd be something funny up with you.' She sent a letter to Mr Maxie Hall, the manager of The Grand, complaining that W.C. Fields was a holy terror, a danger to life and limb and a bad example to the young. Mr Hall didn't bother to reply. He read the letter aloud in Mooney's where, according to Mammy, they all had a good laugh.

'That's not fair,' I said.

'Is that so? And what's not fair about it, Miss?'

'The letter was for him, not the people in the pub.'

'I declare to God. Sometimes you're as bad as she is, d'you know that?'

'No. But—'

'No but nothing! Stop annoying me. I have a headache.'

I decided to run away for good and all because I was fed up getting into trouble and being blamed for everything. I had run away before, plenty of times, but had always got hungry and had had to come home. This time I was going do it properly, with sandwiches.

'But where will you run to?' asked Kathleen when I told her.

'The country.'

It was a Sunday afternoon and she was getting ready to go out, smearing her tan on with damp cotton wool. She hitched up her skirt.

'How does it look? Is it even?'

Her legs had stripes the colour of orange-peel that you find down a sofa.

'No. It's streaky.'

'Ah, sure a galloping horse'll never notice. And what'll you do in the country, love? Providing you get there in the first place.'

'I could sleep in barns and earn money feeding the animals and bringing cows in from fields.'

'Hold on a minute now and let me think.'

She peach-powdered her nose, then flicked the puff over mine with a tickle. 'I'll tell you what: I'm going on a visit and if you're good and do what you're told, you can come along with me.'

'What kind of a visit?'

'Just … to a Home. Now go and wash your hands and face and

comb your hair and we'll be off in two shakes of a mare's tail.'

We stopped at Cully's, where Kathleen bought three big oranges and a Mars bar, and in no time we were sitting upstairs in a number nineteen to Rialto. The sun was shining in and there was a lovely smell off Kathleen, of oranges, mothballs and Californian Poppy perfume.

The bus conductor came swinging along the rail like Errol Flynn. 'Fares, please.'

'One-and-a-half,' said Kathleen, holding out a shilling. 'All the way, please.'

'Certintly, darlin'.'

He clicked two tickets, gave them to me, then leaned down towards Kathleen's head. 'Wouldn't mind going all the way with you meself,' he murmured.

Kathleen looked up with a radiant smile and caught his eye. His expression changed, his chin wobbled. He moved on.

After a while Kathleen took the Mars bar from the bag. 'No more talk of running away now, promise?'

A whole Mars bar for me? I promised.

'Were you ever up it?' she asked as we passed Nelson's Pillar.

'No, were you?'

'Indeed'n I was not. What would the likes of me be doing up that?'

'I don't know. Would you *like* to go up it?'

'Well, I would. And then again I wouldn't because tis high, mighty high, and, although there's a railing, who knows? It could be weak from rust and maybe dangerous.'

'Yeah.'

A small man in the seat in front of us turned around. He removed his black hat and held it against his heart.

'Pardon the interruption, but I couldn't help hearing youse talking about the Pillar and the dangers thereof.'

'Oh?'

'It's well worth it, Miss, the Pillar, if I may be so bold. Oney a tanner and not a thing to be afraid of, no danger whatsoever, the railing being intact and if you folly me, so fully intact, that even if you wanted to take a lep off of it you'd be hard put to, and the view is stupendous on a clear day, oney stupendous and on a *really* clear day, well, you can see from here to …' He waved his hat all over the place. 'The sthairs is tough though, I'll grant you that. A spoiral, you see,' he demonstrated with his hat. 'You do hafta be in the whole of yer health for it. But wanst you're up there—an expee-rience! A real, wanst-in-a-lifetime, honest-to-God, ex-peerience.'

'Imagine that now,' said Kathleen.

'The nipper there'd enjoy it too.'

'I'm sure she would. Thanks very much so.'

'My pleasure, Miss. Good day to you.'

He got off before I could ask if, on a *really* clear day, you could see as far as Mayo.

The bus lurched. Hot, sour bits of Mars came back up but I swallowed them.

'Last stop. Rialto! And the great adventure,' called the conductor and we got off.

Not far from the bus stop there was a huge grey building with bars on every window and a black iron fire-escape zig-zagging up the side. It was as grim as a witch's castle and made me shiver just to look at it. I hoped this wasn't the place for the visit. But it was. My heart sank when we turned into the big front gates. I took hold of Kathleen's hand.

'Is this the Home?'

She nodded with a face that was as tight as a blown-up balloon.

We went in. The air was damp and cold, smelling of old unwanted things: stale bread, rancid butter, mutton stew and musty clothes. We climbed flights of smooth stone steps, passing holy statues with bits missing, noses, ears, toes, fingers and even feet, as if they'd been attacked by some awful disease or a madman with a hammer. The corridors were so dim and green and quiet that it was like walking under water. The deep silence was broken occasionally by distant cries and clatters.

Suddenly, a fat young woman in half a nurse's uniform rushed out of a room, almost knocking us over. She was carrying a covered enamel pail, and belted off holding it well away from her. You knew by her face what was in the pail. And anyway you could smell it.

Kathleen looked down and put her hand on my shoulder. Her face was serious. 'I want you to be a good girl and stay here quietly because I have to see someone now and it's no place for you. I won't be long.'

'Okay.'

'Be good.' She went into the room.

Just as the door was closing a bald old woman sidled up from nowhere.

'That's my gansey,' she shrieked, tearing at my cardigan.

I got the shock of my life. 'No, it's not!'

'Mine!'

Buttons popped as, with surprising strength, she hauled me and the cardigan that my Ma had knitted down the corridor.

Then Kathleen appeared and in no uncertain terms told the woman to get away with herself. The woman giggled, scratched her bald head and scuttled off by the wall.

We picked up the buttons. Kathleen put them into her handbag.

'You'd better come with me so. But keep your lip buttoned, no matter who says what to you.'

The minute I walked into the room, the Mars bar churned. Except for the sweet-sicky smell, it was like walking into a baking-hot oven full of beds and old ladies. The beds had bars like babies' cots and ladies lay in them, crumpled and quiet, like little rag dolls.

Others stood by windows, looking through the bars, in a world of their own; or sat with bird's nests of knitting, unravelling, plucking, worrying the wool; read religious pamphlets; fingered rosary beads; or just waited.

'Look who it is, look!' one screeched, waving at me.

Thinking she knew me from my photograph in the *Sunday Independent* after I won the sack, obstacle *and* egg-and-spoon races in the school sports, I waved and smiled back.

Kathleen gave me a dig. 'Amn't I after telling you? Pay no heed to them oul wans. Now sit here and hould your whisht.'

She put me sitting beside a beaky black-shawled old woman with vicious yellow fingernails curving over her fingertips, who seemed to be asleep with half-closed eyes and open mouth. There wasn't a stir out of her when I sat beside her, but she knew I was there. Don't ask me how I knew, but I did. And she knew that I knew. I knew that too. And she wasn't asleep either because she pick-pick-picked at the quick of her thumb-nail (shredded, bloody, picked to death) with the horny nail of her middle finger.

Kathleen looked nervous. Her cheeks were bright pink. She kept chewing her bottom lip.

'Mother?' she said softly.

The woman's mouth snapped like a rat-trap. Her eyes opened, on me. They were hard and grey, as cold as stones in water.

But why? I hadn't done anything on her. I tried a smile.

The eyes closed.

'How are you today?' Kathleen continued.

There was no reply.

'You're looking well. A bit on the pale side though. Did you get out into the air at all since? Into the garden? I brought you some oranges. Nice sweet ones, I think. Will I peel one for you?'

There was no response. Not even a thanks very much for the oranges.

Kathleen looked at me. 'This is Eily, Mother. Eily Doolin. The little girl I told you about. She's a good girl, Eily. A great help to her Mammy and Daddy.'

'Ouaghh!' Screaming like a savage, the woman jumped up, shoved Kathleen out of the way and, folding her arms tightly around her body, began to stride with great energy up and down the room. With her head thrust forward and her shawls flying back, she was like a big black eagle out hunting its prey.

But whatever about that, what bothered me was that every so often she'd stop in her tracks and pierce me with a look of pure hatred. And I *still* hadn't done anything! Had never even seen her before in my life or spoken to her or even *heard* of her. It wasn't fair. I was always being blamed for things I didn't do. Still and all, she was Kathleen's Ma, so I did my best and the next time she glared, I bared my teeth in a false but friendly smile. Instead of cheering her up, it only made her worse; she clapped a hand over her mouth and groaned as if in mortal agony.

Kathleen, all concern, went to her aid. She knocked Kathleen over and, howling like a banshee, descended on me. I was scooped up and shaken till the teeth rattled in my head and my neck felt broken. Then she flung me to the floor and kicked me.

'Bastard, bastard, get that bastard out of here,' she kept screaming, her face purple, white foaming from her mouth.

When Kathleen rushed to rescue me, her mother straightened up and drove the crook of her elbow into her stomach.

'You slut! Bitch! Get out of my house. I rue the day you were born. Never let me lay eyes on you again, you whore!' Spitting down at me. 'And take your father's melt with you!'

Nurses flew in and held her down. Old ladies cackled and chuckled as if it was a Laurel-and-Hardy.

'It's alright, love, it's alright, it's all over now,' Kathleen kept whispering as we limped along the corridor.

'But what did I do, Kathleen? What?'

'Nothing. You did nothing, love. You don't have to. It's just … People sometimes get the wrong end of the stick.'

She unlocked a heavy door and we stepped out onto one of the landings of the fire-escape. The air was clean and cool.

'Ah, sure look at you, God love you.' She spat on her hankie and cleaned my face. 'She scratched you too, did she? The oul rip! I'll not forgive this. No. She's gone beyond the beyonds this time. There's no going back now. Listen to me, alannah, you'll be alright here for a couple of minutes—as safe as houses. There's something I have to attend to before we go. I won't be long. You can see the mountains from here, look. I'll only be a tick.'

She closed the door behind her.

I looked at the mountains, mauve and brown and very far away. They started to shimmer, so I looked down through the lacy iron-work to the gardens below. Then they started to shimmer. My head got light, my legs weak, and vomit shot from me like a bullet down into a bed of decaying roses. An old man on a seat nearby never knew how lucky he was. After a while two crows landed in the rose-bed and began pecking around.

Then the door opened and a boy of about my own age, with brown hair, was pushed out beside me. We pretended not to notice each other. He was wearing brown corduroy trousers, a white shirt with the collar flattened down, a Fair Isle pullover, fallen-down grey knee socks and Clark's sandals. His eyelashes were long and his neck was clean.

'Do you have to get glasses?' he asked suddenly.

'What?'

'Glasses.'

'No, why? Do you?'

He shook his head sadly. 'No.'

I was puzzled. Then I asked if he'd *like* to get glasses and he said

no, because they'd all call him Specky-four-eyes, as well as everything else. I was about to ask what other names they called him
when a woman started moaning on the far side of the door.

'Tony oh Tony love Tony.'

The boy gasped. He took a Sailor's Chu from his pocket, broke
it in two and offered me half.

'Thanks very much,' I said, although I hated Sailor's Chu.

'Tony love oh Tony, help me.'

She was trying to get the door to open.

Tears filled the boy's eyes. His mouth began to tremble.

'I had a whole Mars bar coming over on the bus,' I said to cheer
him up.

'What bus?'

'The nineteen.'

'Oh.'

'They're my favourite. Well, second favourites, after Sailor's Chu.'

The woman was scrabbling at the door like a rat in a biscuit tin.

'The only thing about them is they're fourpence.' I spoke loudly to cover the noise.

He nodded miserably.

'How much do you get a week?'

'A shilling,' he whispered.

'A shilling? You're lucky! I only get sixpence. Fourpence for the
flicks and a two-penny Honeycap. You're dead lucky so you are!'

'I know.'

Other voices came. I couldn't think of anything else to say, so we
listened as the woman, sobbing, was dragged away.

I remembered the mountains. 'They're nice, aren't they?'

'What are?'

'The mountains.'

Before he could answer, the door opened and a young man stuck
his head out.

'Come on you.'

The boy looked at me. 'Cheerio.'

'Cheerio. Thanks for the bar.'

I watched him through the railings, trotting behind the young man, who strode along fiercely, as if he couldn't get away quickly enough. I didn't blame him. When he reached the gate, the boy turned and looked back at the Home. I waved; but he mustn't have seen me.

I got rid of the Sailor's Chu. The old man on the seat made his way over to where it fell. He poked at it, stabbed it with the point of his stick, and put it in his pocket. Then he danced with glee like Fred Astaire gone wrong. A stout nurse appeared with a wheel-chair, popped him into it and wheeled him away like a baby.

A cold wind started up and the mountains got purple. Then Kathleen came out with her face damp, her nose and eyes red and shiny.

'Are you alright, Kathleen, are you?'

Saying nothing, she wrapped her arms around me, holding me so closely against her that I could feel the softness and warmth of her. It was lovely. I wanted to stay like that forever, safe and happy.

'We're going now, love. For good and all. Sooner or later every-thing ends. And do you know what I'm thinking?'

'No.'

'That we'll treat ourselves to a little something when we get into town. To cheer ourselves up, after our trials and tribulations.' She smiled. 'Do you think we deserve it?'

'I do.'

Wynn's Hotel in Abbey Street was our destination. It was full of jovial priests drinking whiskey and smoking like chimneys. We had an afternoon tea of thin ham sandwiches with the crusts cut off, hot scones with butter and jam, chocolate Swiss Roll, cream horns and tea from a real silver pot. It was beautiful.

★

One night when my parents were at the pictures, Kathleen asked me to sing a song. She seemed to be out of sorts so I sang her favourite, 'Red River Valley', and didn't know what was up when she hugged me tightly with the tears running down her face. When I asked what was wrong, she shook her head, saying it was nothing, nothing, nothing at all, but couldn't talk.

Next day when I came home from school, her room was bare and she was gone. Mammy hadn't been satisfied with her.

A few months later a postcard came for me from Philadelphia. She said she missed me more than words could say and was working hard in her second cousin's pub.

I missed Kathleen too and under the blankets cried and prayed that the Yanks would be able to straighten out her lovely cornflower eyes.

ANOTHER JEWISH PLOT

U ncle Jack and Auntie Sue lived one door away, on the other side of Madam Butterfly. They weren't our real uncle and auntie. Everyone just called them that because they hadn't any children of their own; though they seemed to like children well enough and never gave us the bum's rush or threatened us with police for playing ball in the lane against the wall of their house.

Their front garden was as proper as the Protestants', with no dockleaves, dandelions or daisies. There were no flowers either, just bright green grass, a monkey-puzzle tree with dark-green stiffish leaves and a neatly clipped yellow privet hedge.

The day I made my First Holy Communion I called in to let them see me. They stood at their door admiring me, then gave me a holy picture of Our Lady of Good Counsel with their names and the date on the back.

May 1947
In memory of your First Holy Communion.
Pray for Auntie Sue & Uncle Jack.

'How much didja get there?' asked Gracie Fox, rattling her bag of half-crowns.

'Nothing.'

'What?'

'A holy picture.'

'A *what?*'

'You heard me.'

'Well, Ikey Mo! What d'you expect? Saving his dough. Give us a gander.' She took a look, tossed her veil in contempt. 'Wouldn't be bothered with that. Give us the money any day.'

I heard the women that night over glasses of port.

'A holy *picture,*' Mrs Ryder was horrified. 'I don't *believe* it!'

'It's true,' replied Mammy. 'True as I'm sitting here.'

'Well, you know what they're like,' said Gracie Fox's Ma. 'That crowd.'

They knew. There was a silence while they sipped their port.

'A bloody holy picture, God forgive me,' burst out Mrs Ryder. 'When I *think* of it. The *cheek.*'

'No more than thrupence in Cully's.'

'Well, you know what they say,' said Mammy.

'We do.'

'And there's no smoke without fire.'

'True for you, Mrs Doolin.'

'Ah, they'd live in your ear that crowd.'

'They would.'

'Yeah. And sell the wax for candles.'

I drifted back to sleep wondering what sort of a crowd would live in your ear and why they'd want to.

Mammy didn't like Uncle Jack because he wore galoshes over his shoes on wet days. There was something funny, she said, something *sissyish*, about galoshes. And any man who wore them.

I didn't think Uncle Jack was a sissy but had enough cop-on not to say so. And galoshes seemed like a good idea to me; much better than a wad of newspaper that soaked up the rain when you had holey soles; but again I kept quiet.

He was a tall baker, Uncle Jack, who worked in Johnston

Mooney and O'Brien's Bakery in Ball's Bridge. His skin and thick brown hair were always hazed in a silky film of fine white flour. He rode an old-fashioned bike (Mammy hated men on bikes), a real upstairs model, with a Sturmey-Archer gear, a dynamo and cable brakes. You'd hear him before you saw him, whistling 'Pedro the Fisherman', sailing along on his high bike, like a happy king.

Auntie Sue was quiet and kept herself to herself. The women called her crafty and plain as a pikestaff with those teeth (buck) and the glasses (milk-bottle bottoms). Mrs Fox couldn't understand for the life of her what *he*, being handsome enough in his own way, had ever seen in her.

In the house Auntie Sue always wore starchy aprons which she made herself by hand from white linen. I thought they were lovely, crisp and clean. Mammy said they made her look like a Fullers' waitress. On account of being foreign, she spoke with a funny accent. Her long, straight hair, as sleek and shiny as a blackbird's wing, was coiled into a bun on the back of her neck. Mrs Fox, who was a hairdresser before she got married, was of the opinion that a Marcel perm would've improved matters, but Mrs Ryder said she was too tight to part with the spondulicks.

You got used to the buck teeth after a while.

I never saw Auntie Sue with a coat or hat on, gossiping with the women, going to the pictures, or into town. She spent her days cleaning, polishing, gardening, cooking dinners, baking cakes and making aprons and liked being occupied because the devil makes work for idle hands.

We were playing 'Queeny-aye-oh' in the lane one day when the ball went over the wall. I was sent to fetch it and was trying to wipe my sticky pawmarks off the shiny letterbox when the door opened.

'Eily.'

I liked the way she said it: Ellie. It made me think I was somebody else.

[63]

'Sorry, Auntie Sue, but the ball went over the wall.'

'Come, please, and look for it yourself.'

I wiped my feet on a mat marked 'Welcome' and followed her down the hall. Two lovely smells came into my nose: lavender from a spiky jugful, and the other I couldn't identify except that it was spicy and warm, like Christmas. Later, Auntie Sue explained that she hung clove-spiked oranges by every window so that the summer breeze, wafting through, would make the house fragrant.

We went through the kitchen, bright with copper pans, into the back garden full of bachelor's buttons, pansies, petunias, carnations, love-in-a-mist, marguerites, lavender, and lilies. Gladioli leaned on slim canes. Roses, sweet pea and apple trees clambered along the walls. There were lettuces in a patch with scallions, radishes, rosemary, parsley and thyme. Islands of paving stone had white and purple flowers curling around their edges.

The marmalade cat, Ginger, rested on a green cushion under a table. He half-opened one tiger eye, took a look at me, sniffed the air, stood up, turned around twice and plumped himself down again.

'He's lovely.'

'Ginger.'

'He walks along our wall sometimes.'

'Ginger by name if not by nature. You look hot.'

'I am, yeah, roasting.'

'Like some lemonade?

'Yes, please. I'm sweating.'

'You'd better find the ball for your friends first. They seem impatient.'

I found the ball in a clump of candytuft and flung it back over to the gang. Ginger sniffed at my sandal. Then Auntie Sue came out with a tray on which there was a jug of lemonade, two tall glasses and a plate of cake. She suggested I might like to wash my hands before eating, so I did, in the kitchen, with blue soap that smelled of hyacinths.

'That's lovely lemonade,' I said, after swallowing a glassful in one go.

She poured more. 'I'm glad you like it. Just lemons and sugar. Now, perhaps I can invite you,' offering it as politely as if I was a grown-up, 'to some carrot cake?'

Carrot cake? I made a face. I hated carrots. And who ever heard of making a cake from carrots? Not wanting to hurt her feelings, I said a small bit. And it was lovely. Crumbly and nutty, not tasting of carrots at all but sweetly, of cake.

She smiled at my surprise. 'Almonds, eggs, sugar and naturally, carrots. But no flour.'

'I didn't know you could have a cake with no flour.'

'Oh yes. Think of meringue.'

My eyes lit up.

'You like meringue?'

'Yes.'

'No flour. Just egg white and sugar, a strong wrist to beat and the time to cook slow.'

Halfway through my second piece of cake, Madam Butterfly, next door, began playing the piano. Auntie Sue leaned back listening with obvious pleasure.

'Chopin. A delight. We're fortunate our neighbour is such a pianist, yes?'

I smiled. 'Yes.'

But I was surprised; when Mammy heard Madam Butterfly, she'd raise her eyes to heaven. 'Jesus Christ, she's at it *again*. Is there no bloody peace? She'll drive me mad if she doesn't stop that racket.' She'd tell Daddy to be a man, to go in and put his foot down. But he liked Madam Butterfly *and* her piano, and anyway it wasn't *his* battle.

At night, I prayed for a bolt of lightning to strike the piano so's Mammy wouldn't end up in Grangegorman with all the mad people.

'Are you fond of music?' asked Auntie Sue.

'Yeah, tap-dancing music. I used to learn ballet but now I learn tap and I love it.'

Her eyes twinkled behind her glasses. 'Perhaps you'll do a dance for me some day?'

'A dance is called a *routine* in tap,' I explained. 'I could do one now if you like.'

I did the 'Me and My Shadow' routine on a paving slab among the flowers. But I wasn't any good because you need the taps and anyway, I couldn't hear myself singing with all the hooting and mocking from my pals in the lane. Doing your dance for Ikey Mo, they jeered later.

Auntie Sue applauded when I was finished. She said I was an expressive dancer and could bring my tap-shoes in any time and dance for her. So I did; in my new red tap-shoes with the satin ribbons I danced for hours among the flowers, pretending that Ginger was a Hollywood talent scout as he sat regarding me with cool interest from a distance.

Uncle Jack thought I was terrific too, as good as Ginger Rogers if I practised.

I was delighted; Mammy always said I was too heavy on my feet to ever be any good.

Auntie Sue was nice because she always had time to listen and took what you had to say seriously. I told her about our school and my pals and any trouble I was in. No matter what, I knew Auntie Sue would never tell anyone or laugh in my face and say I was stupid or imagining things.

'You're not to be going *in* there,' my Ma said one day. 'I don't want you *in* there. Stay out and play with your pals or come in and go to bed, take your pick. But stay out of *that house*.'

'But—'

'But nothing.'

'Why?'

'That's why. Because I say so. Now stop asking questions and do as you're told.'

D.J. was bawling fit to burst. Mammy shot the last of the gripe water into him. His eyes opened in shock but he had it swallowed before he knew what hit him. Then he was off again. I got nabbed before I could escape.

'Bring him out for a walk like a good girl. Down to the chemist. Get a large bottle of gripe water. Tell him to put it on the bill.'

On the way back Auntie Sue was cleaning her brasses. I wheeled D.J. up to let her see him, even though he was still bawling. She leaned towards him, lifted her little finger and, humming softly, held it in front of him, moving it gently from side to side. After a moment D.J. began to watch the finger like a hawk. He frowned and blinked. His own fingers began twitching like chubby pink worms. Then he stopped crying, gulped and grinned foolishly on one side of his face like Daddy on Saturdays in from the pub.

'He's smiling, Auntie Sue!'

'Who's a lovely little fella?' said Auntie Sue.

'You're making him smile.'

'A lovely smile. And blue eyes like his big sister. Would you like me to knit you a little jumper, eh, D.J.? To go with your lovely blue eyes? What do you say to that, eh?

As if he thought it was a great idea, D.J. grinned then, on the other side of his face. It was so funny, I had to laugh.

'... and she made him stop crying just by holding up her little finger and singing a song. Just by holding up her finger like that, look, and he smiled, Mammy. D.J. smiled. And she's going to knit him a jumper to go with his eyes and—'

'She needn't bother,' snapped Mammy. 'She needn't bother her barney with any jumpers. Blue or otherwise. And what're you doing in there again anyway after what I told you? Time and time again!

I'm blue in the face telling you to stay *out* of that house and *away* from those people.'

'But—'

'And don't argue!'

★

One day I was skating down the road when I met Uncle Jack coming up pushing his bike.

'What's up?'

'A puncture.'

'Oh yeah, you have alright.'

'We all have our troubles by the sound of it.'

'How do you mean?'

'Well, those skates, do you never give them a drop of oil?'

'We haven't got any oil.'

'Come in so and I'll see if we can fix you up.'

His shed at the bottom of the garden had shelves along the walls and a tidy workbench. Boxes labelled 'SCREW', 'NUT' and 'NAIL' were stacked alongside larger ones, 'CLAMP', 'HAMMER', 'SCREW-DRIVER (ASSORTED)'. Wondering if there was only one nail in 'NAIL', I opened it and found, not the dried-up orange rinds, dust and rusty hairpins in my Da's toolbox, but nails of different sizes in red rubber bands.

'We'll attend to the skates first,' said Uncle Jack, taking an oil-can with a curving spout from the workbench. Ginger strolled in and watched the proceedings with a bored expression, as if he had nothing better to do. I sang 'Over the Rainbow' because Uncle Jack liked it and he was like the Tin Man with his curly oil-can.

'That should do the trick now,' he said, flicking his finger on the wheels until they spun like silk and fast as a train.

Then we mended the puncture. I filled a basin with water from the garden tap and put it on the ground beside the upturned bike.

From 'WRENCH' I produced two and from 'BICYCLE REPAIR KIT' a skinny yellow tin. With the help of the wrenches, we whipped off the tyre in no time.

'Much better than forks,' I observed.

'How do you mean?'

'For getting the tyre off, and anyway forks go all bendy and you can't aim at your dinner properly. My Ma's always giving out.'

He thought for a moment. 'It's important to have the right tool, Eily. The right tool for the job is all-important.'

I pressed the tube into the water until bubbles rose. 'That's it. There's the lad's the cause of the trouble.' He lifted the tube from the water. I dried it in white linen rags. With a bit of gritty sand-paper he rubbed at the area with the hole. I chose a sound patch. He applied rubber solution. I stuck the patch over the hole and held it down.

'My Da has a bike too, with a saddle on the crossbar for when I was small, but he doesn't go on it now. Mammy'd like a car but she doesn't know the meaning of the word afford. It's in the coal-house, all rusty, with the tyres as flat as pancakes.'

The thought of Daddy's bike dumped in with the coal, slack and spiders made me sad.

'Maybe we could fix it up for him,' said Uncle Jack.

'That'd be rare.'

But I wasn't so sure; Mammy was tired of men in berets (Daddy always wore a beret on a bike) with bicycle-clips on their trousers.

Uncle Jack checked that the patch was dry before grating French chalk over it. Then we put all the tools away, gave the bike a good pump up and set it on its wheels all ready for the road again.

I explained that Mammy used French chalk too, to mark mate-rial when she was dressmaking, and he was interested in that.

'Come and have a drink,' called Auntie Sue, from under a yellow sunshade.

As I ran in to wash my hands, I saw her folding something blue into a piece of pink tissue-paper. I wondered what it was and thought I knew, but didn't like to ask. I had lemonade, they drank tea and we all ate crispy *langues de chat*, French for cat's tongues. The tissue-wrapped parcel was on a chair next to mine. I tried not to look at it.

'Do you know what that is?' asked Auntie Sue.

'No.'

'Guess.'

I touched it. 'It's soft.'

'It is.'

'And blue.'

'Yes?'

'And small.'

'You're warm.'

'I give up!'

'But you're warm.'

'I do.'

'Well, close your eyes.'

I closed my eyes, and it was D.J.'s jumper. 'I knew it was, I knew! Look, Uncle Jack, it's for D.J., a jumper! Isn't it lovely?'

It was blue like his eyes, with a cluster of daisies embroidered in white silk thread on the left shoulder.

'Do you think he'll like it?' asked Uncle Jack.

We laughed.

Ginger miaowed to say he didn't like being left out. Auntie Sue bent with a saucer of milk. She was straightening up when someone hammered on the front door. We all jumped with the fright, but no one moved.

'Will I go?' I said after a moment.

'It's alright,' said Uncle Jack, who had his hand over one of Auntie Sue's. 'I'll do it.'

'I got an awful fright,' I said when he had gone. 'Did you?'

She nodded, but didn't look at me. Her face was white.

'I nearly jumped out of my skin,' I said.

She took the parcel from the chair and smoothed the tissue paper with slow strokes as if to calm herself. Her head was bent. Strands of silver shone in her hair.

Then my Ma had me by the arm. 'I've been looking everywhere for you for the last half-hour. You had me worried sick. Sick. Amn't I always telling you not to—' She stopped, looked at Auntie Sue and put on a sweet voice. 'I'm always telling her not to be coming in here annoying you.'

'But Eily doesn't annoy us. Not in the least. We're happy to see her, in fact, because—'

'Yes, well, but I'm her mother and know what's best and I'd prefer it if she stayed out playing with her own pals. It's more natural if you understand what I mean. Come along!' She jerked my arm nearly out of its socket.

'But Mammy—'

'That's enough out of you!'

'She knitted a jumper. A jumper for D.J. with daisies. Show her, Auntie Sue! Wait till you see it, Mammy, it's lovely!'

Auntie Sue unwrapped the tissue and produced the little blue jumper.

Mammy barely looked at it. Her face was pink, her grip ferocious. 'Thanks very much but I wouldn't dream of it. The house is *full* of jumpers, full, more than we know what to do with. Why not give it to one of your own? Say goodbye now, Eily.'

She dragged me home saying I was the boldest, brassiest, most disobedient girl she had ever come across and wasn't she always telling me? and how many times would she have to? and I'd have her in Grangegorman by the time I was finished.

When she ran out of steam, I asked her why.

She lit another cigarette, spooned a milky mush of arrowroot biscuits into D.J.'s bottle, then made a bigger hole in the teat with a darning-needle held over the gas.

'She isn't your auntie anyway in the first place.'

'I know that, but—'

'And stop biting your nails. You'll be sorry when you're big.' She sighed. 'I just don't want you going *in* there, Eily, that's all. Neither does Daddy. So be good, do what you're told and don't be always getting yourself into trouble. Now run down to Cully's for twenty Gold Flake and a box of matches. They're different, not our kind. You're too young to understand, but you will in time. Different from we are. You can keep the penny change.'

Sometimes at night I used to wonder what Auntie Sue would do with the jumper because D.J. was the only baby she knew.

★

We moved to a bigger house in a different neighbourhood. Five years later, one winter's day, Gracie Fox told me in school that Auntie Sue had died.

'Who?'

'Ah remember! Ikey Mo! Our First Communion and the holy picture. I'll never forget your face. You were disgusted.' She laughed.

I remembered. 'When did she die?'

'A while back.'

'What did she die of?'

'I haven't a clue. As far as I know she just died.'

My parents had seen the death notice in the paper but hadn't bothered to mention it.

'Didn't think you'd be interested,' said my mother.

A couple of weeks later I called up to see Uncle Jack, afraid that he might have forgotten me, as I had forgotten them.

The door brasses were mottled with grime. They hadn't been

polished for ages. Just when I was thinking there was no one at home, the door opened and Uncle Jack peered out.

'Yes?'

I was shocked to see how old he had become.

'Hello, Uncle Jack. It's me. Eily Doolin. I used to live—'

'Eily, is it?' His face lit up. 'Ah, Eily. Eily, child, come in, come in. I'm glad to see you. It's your voice I recognise.'

There was a newspaper spread on the dining-room table and an old Jacob's biscuit tin with 'SHOE POLISHES. BLACK, OX-BLOOD, NIGGER-BROWN' in faded lettering.

'I was just giving the shoes a polish.'

His voice had lost its strength, his thick hair had become sparse and his skin was as thin as paper. He told me he had cataracts in both eyes that would need operations when they were ready.

'Who? The doctors?'

'No. The cataracts. I'm told they have to get to a certain stage before they can operate.'

'They have to get worse before they get better?'

'Exactly,' he smiled. 'You hit the nail on the head there. And now tell me all, Eily. How are your parents?'

He listened with interest to everything I had to say, about where we lived, the people, my family, school, teachers, everything.

'And the dancing?' he asked when I had finished.

'I gave it up.'

'You didn't.'

'I did.'

'That's a shame.'

'I wasn't good enough.'

'For what?'

'Too heavy on my feet.'

'You were good enough for us, so you were. A grand little dancer.'

We sat for a while without speaking, looking into the bright coal fire. It was late afternoon. The room was getting dark. I looked around but there was no sign, sight, or sound of Ginger.

Then we both started talking at the same time, but he, seeming not to notice, continued. It was about Auntie Sue. He wanted to tell me, to explain so that I would understand.

Because she had been a Jewish woman who had married him, a Catholic, Auntie Sue's family had disowned her, closed their doors to her, banished her forever from their company. She was dead to them. The dear friend of her youth, a woman called Bella Weil, and many of her beloved relations had died in Hitler's concentration camps. They both loved children but were unable to have any. The authorities refused to let them adopt. He had lost his faith. The people blamed her. It was another plot, he said, another diabolical Jewish plot.

I didn't know what he meant.

'She was fond of you, Eily. You made her laugh with your talk and your company and the dancing of course. She often wondered if you had kept it up. Yes, she was fond of you and missed you when … ah, don't, love, don't cry. Not for her. Isn't she in a better place now?'

We had tea, bread and butter and seedy cake that had got a bit stale.

Before I left, he took a brown paper parcel from a drawer and gave it to me. I opened it in the bus. Wrapped in pink tissue there were three white linen aprons with my initials embroidered in blue silk thread in the top left-hand corner.

Uncle Jack died soon afterwards. At his funeral, on a bleak December day, the women agreed that it was a crying shame that they hadn't been able to get the priest in before it was too late.

THE BOY
WHO THOUGHT
HE WAS A TRAIN

'You know who loses babies?' asked Itchy.

'Who?'

'Spaghetti.'

'Babies?'

'Yeah.'

'Whose babies?'

'Her own.'

'She hasn't got any.'

'I know. Because she loses them.'

'Only Danny and he's not a baby.'

'Are you gone deaf? I'm after telling you. She *loses* them.'

'Where?'

'How do I know? An' if you knew they wouldn't be lost.'

'But how could you lose a baby?'

Itchy shrugged.

'Say you took one out in its pram and went into a shop for a message. It'd still be there when you came out, wouldn't it?'

'Don't know and I care less.'

I asked my Da but he rattled the paper. It wasn't his department.

The Flynns lived over the road, next door to the Ryders. Mrs Flynn was Spaghetti behind her back because she was an Ey-tie. Her husband, Mr Flynn, was a roguish man with a roving eye, a butcher in Moore Street. They had one child, Danny, the boy who thought he was a train.

Danny thought he was the Cork Express: he chugged up and down the road three times a day, at ten in the morning, five-past-two after dinner, and five-past-seven after tea. You could set your watch, if you had a watch, by Danny. Whatever the weather, be it stormy, snowy, a heat wave, or Christmas Day when no one went out except for Mass or a walk after the turkey, he'd be there at his time, chugging along, taking on water, letting off steam.

'If the buses were as reliable as Danny, we'd all be quids in,' Daddy said once and we laughed because it was true.

The school wouldn't take Danny because he was simple and couldn't talk. He never looked to the right or the left or spoke to anyone, just kept full steam ahead as if no one existed. Blarney Park didn't mind; we were used to him; didn't even mind when the Halpins' Ford Prefect burst into flames with Mr Halpin *underneath* and Danny puffed calmly by like a well-oiled engine should, just as if people weren't flinging buckets of water on Mr Halpin and beating him with dusty doormats.

Sometimes, small children who didn't know any better joined on behind to make the train longer, but he'd get rid of them quickly enough by staying in one place going '*chu*-chu-chu-chu, *chu*-chu-chu-chu, *chu*-chu-chu-chu, *chu*-chu-chu-chu,' until they got fed up and wandered away. Then, all business, he'd resume his schedule.

Once, this huge American soldier with a scaldy crew cut came sauntering up the road as if he owned the place. He stopped and stared at Danny, who was letting off steam outside the Widow's.

'Hey, kid! Yew happena know the Shaughnessys live around here?'

Danny didn't even look at him. He continued with the steam, then changed his noise and began to take on water.

The American's face reddened. His crew cut glinted in the sun like stubble in a cornfield. He pulled out a packet of Wrigley's Juicy Fruit and shoved it rudely into Danny's face. 'I assed a question. Yew deaf?'

Danny blinked once, then stoked up his engine and took off smoothly, gathering speed as he went, obliging the American to step out of his way. He glared after Danny with pale furious eyes. 'Nutty as a fruitcake,' he muttered to no one in particular.

I made sure of the chewing-gum before I showed him the O'Shaughnessys' house.

Danny looked like a pixie with his golden skin, sooty eyes and pointy ears. He was small for his age. 'Thirteen? Hah! Looks more like ten to me. Of course we all know why *that* is!' The opinion of the Blarney Park women was that Danny was underdeveloped because his Ma (Spaghetti) was an Ey-tie who didn't cook potatoes.

I thought Mrs Flynn was lovely, easily the nicest on the road (except sometimes the Widow with her war-paint on). She had black curly hair, velvety, purple pansy eyes, red lips and no stockings on her slim brown legs. We were all playing 'Relievio' one summer's night when she came out in a red taffeta frock and high-heels, with a red rose in her hair. We stared. Mousey Heron and the big boys fidgeted in their trousers.

'Come on, come on,' growled Mousey, in a tough voice. 'On with the game!'

Mrs Ryder, out sweeping in her apron, leaned on her sweeping-brush, looking after the swishy frock.

'Hm! *Some* people around here seem to think they're Rita Hayworth all of a sudden,' she said with a sour face.

'Mrs Flynn is nicer,' I said. 'She has a smaller mouth.'

Mrs Ryder rolled her fag from one side to the other, spat it out, stamped on it, then lifted her brush and banged it on the ground. 'And what in God's holy name would you know about it, Eily Doolin, you little know-all, and you only a child.' She barged into her house and slammed the door.

Mr Flynn wasn't a good husband for a woman to have. Everyone knew that. He drank and went with other women, I don't know where. One Sunday up at Collinstown watching airplanes, we saw him drinking stout with a lady in a fur coat like Lana Turner. 'On a Sunday too,' muttered Mammy, her face as red as her hat. 'That man has no shame.' Daddy was all on to join them but Mammy said under no circumstances and that she'd rather be seen dead in the back of a ditch than in the company of a peroxide brasser like that.

The women liked Mr Flynn. They only pretended not to. He had big shoulders, curly chestnut hair with a matching moustache and eyes as bluey-green as the sea when it's sunny. Once, when I was crying, he scooped me up and swirled me over his head as if he was God or Superman until I was screaming with the laughing, begging him to stop, but he didn't and, when he did, I was sorry and wanted him to do it again.

I loved watching him creep up quietly, like a wolf, on a huddle of chatting women, as if they were lambs to be pounced on and devoured with his strong white teeth. And when he did pounce, they loved it. You could see it a mile off. 'Oh, you're awful, Mick Flynn!' Squealing and poking, all girlish and giggly. 'Stop it now stop, you're a terrible man.' He'd wrap his strong fingers around, squeezing softly, high under their arms. 'Come here to me, ladies, till I tell you.'

He'd whisper in his husky rough voice until, delighted and laughing like drains, they'd murder him with their mops, bits of old vest and feather-dusters, then run away in to the haven of their homes.

Even though Danny was his only child, Mr Flynn had no time for him; he never brought him fishing up the canal, or to the Botanics, the Phoenix Park or Dalymount for a match, or anywhere. In fact, he never looked at Danny when he was out or spoke to him at all. And Danny never looked at him.

At least one of Mr Flynn's fingers was always encased in a raggedy bandage or bloody Elastoplast. His suit was in tatters from falling over his shadow, drunk. 'We shall rise again,' you'd hear, in the middle of the night. 'We shall rise!' And when you looked out the window, he'd be sprawled on the ground, unable to get up. Then, with her coat on over her nightie, Mrs Flynn would hurry out to help him. He'd slobber over her, kissing and mauling her, then turn nasty and maybe take a swing at her and end up crying about how sorry he was and what a useless bloody fucker into the bargain.

Later, from their house, there'd be shouting, noise and cries so awful that you'd have to pull the blankets over your head and pretend not to hear.

One autumn day, when leaves were flying, Mrs Flynn asked me to run down to the Monument Creamery for two ounces of butter and three hot-buttered eggs. It was a long way to go for such a small message, but I went and when I came back she brought me into the sitting-room and gave me a dish of ice-cream that she had made herself. It was the nicest ice-cream I had ever eaten: soft, pale-pink, tasting of warm summer berries.

'Gelato. At home we say gelato.' Her voice was gentle. 'You say it, Eily.'

'Gel-atto.'

'Si! That's good.'

'I didn't know you could make ice-cream in a house.'

We went into the kitchen where she showed me the ice-cream-maker, a big bowl with a lid and a paddle sticking out.

'To stir. You got to stir. To make it … no lumpsa.' She touched my cheek. 'Make it smooth. Like your skeen.'

She explained that the ice-cream-maker had come with her all the way from Italy because her husband had always loved her ice-cream. Her smile was lovely, but sad.

'It's old now,' she said. 'Antique. But good ice-cream, si?'

Just when I was going to ask her all about Italy, she clasped her hand over her mouth, hurried from the kitchen and ran upstairs.

I could hear her getting sick in the bathroom.

Unsure of what to do, I waited for a minute or so. Then decided to go.

In the hall a sudden, rackety clatter from the dining-room made me look in. Danny was there, on the floor with hundreds of coloured building-blocks, rocking, keening softly, his arms folded tightly around his body.

'Hello, Danny,' I said, talking to him for the first time in my life because I was in his house. 'Building a castle are you?' Though I could see that he wasn't. 'I'll give you a hand. I'm great at building.'

I don't know why I said that but, anyway, I did, and sat down opposite him on the cold, cracked lino.

The room was bare and dull. Wet turf seeped in the fireplace, giving out nothing but slow grey smoke. The walls were empty of the usual pictures of lightly draped ladies with urns on their shoulders, olden-day people getting married with stern faces, or what-nots with dainty ornaments and stuff like that. There was a dining-table with four tucked-in chairs, two fireside chairs and a sideboard with one of the doors missing. The lino had patches of burn that gave off a smell.

My Grandpa had given me a present of a little cloth doll called Una from the Isle of Man. I took her out of my pocket, put her on the floor and began to build a castle around her, telling a story about her at the same time. The bigger the castle got, with turrets, dungeons, and secret passages, the more exciting the story became. I soon forgot everything and was concerned only with the helpless princess, the prince and their struggle against the monster that was out to destroy them.

The Angelus bell brought me back to real life. The room had got dark and to my surprise, in the glow from the fire, now burning brightly, I saw Danny's eyes, shining with excitement, on me.

'I'm going,' I said.

He threw back his head and howled like a wolf in a forest.

I was astonished. 'But I have to. My tea'll be ready. I'll be murdered if I'm late.'

I reached for my doll. But Danny's hand flicked out like a snake's tongue, scooped up the doll and shoved it up his sleeve. Then he curled up as tightly as a hedgehog.

'Gimme my doll!'

He wouldn't, so I had to try to get it. I pushed him, punched, stuck fingers into his soft bits, pulled hair, took a running jump on top, to knock him over, but he was as strong as the Rock of Gibraltar.

'You louser, you dirty louser, Danny Flynn. Gimme my doll,' I screamed. A gleam of bare skin on the back of his neck; I was baring my teeth for a bite when Mrs Flynn came rushing in.

'No, Eily, no, stop.'

'Well he has my doll and he won't give it back.'

'Your *doll*?'

'Yeah, up his sleeve. My Grandpa gave it to me.'

'Danny has your—'

'Doll, yeah, from the Isle of Man, and it's mine.'

'Momento, Eily. One moment please.'

She hunkered down to Danny and, murmuring in Italian as sweet and soft as music, began to stroke his head.

He groaned, looking for sympathy, the sneaky little canat. I know what I'd have given him. My foot itched for another kick.

After a while Mrs Flynn stood up and gave me a look of reassurance. But I didn't trust Danny any further than I could throw him, so I kept a poker-face.

He uncurled himself into a crouch and leaned towards me.

'Gimme my doll,' I said.

His mouth opened. His face got red. Blue veins like thin worms bulged in the sides of his forehead. Sounds in the shape of words came from his throat. He was trying to say something, but I didn't know what.

'He wants you ...' Mrs Flynn explained, after a silence. 'He'd like to hear the end of your story.'

'He would?' I was astonished.

Danny grunted. Yes.

I nearly laughed. People were always telling me to shut up and keep quiet; that I'd talk the hind legs off a dead donkey, was a terrible chatterbox, and had an overwrought imagination.

'But I can't,' I said, feeling sorry. 'My tea'll be ready.'

'Well, perhaps ... tomorrow?'

'We're back to school. The holidays are over tomorrow.'

The light went out of Danny's eyes. He looked away, started to rock again.

I thought of him being the train or sitting there all by himself, with no one to play with or talk to, building castles and knocking them down.

'I'll tell you what,' I said to him. 'We'll strike a bargain. If you give me my doll now, I'll come in after school tomorrow and finish the story for you. I swear I will. Cross my heart and hope to die if I don't. That's fair, isn't it? Isn't it, Danny? And fair play is bonny play.'

★

By the time the Christmas holidays were coming I had told Danny all the stories I knew and more besides. I went in every day after school (except hockey day) and always found him ready and waiting with the blocks. He began to say things too, now and then, and I got to be able to understand him.

My pals said we kissed and my Ma didn't know why I was wasting my time with such a hopeless case. But I didn't mind. I liked telling stories to Danny because he listened.

When I ran out of real ones, I made up my own and these were the stories that Danny loved best. Well, my kingdoms were bigger, my witches wickeder, my monsters more evil and my princesses purer, poorer and more beautiful than ordinary book ones. It was Danny's idea to make the building-blocks our characters. He moved them about as the story demanded and never got mixed up or forgot which was which.

I began to think that maybe he wasn't as simple as he was made out to be.

There was a monster baddie in every story that had to be destroyed and the killing was Danny's big moment. He'd kneel up, gripping the poker, eyes bright with valour, a knight in shining armour. 'The monster must *die*!' I'd command. Down would come the poker, killing the monster once and for all, wiping it off the face of the earth, giving the people their freedom. Then, with great vim and vigour, we'd rout the whole kingdom, shouting with glee, 'We're free, we're free', until his Ma came in to calm us with cocoa.

One day I was keeping D.J. quiet while Mammy, who was a dressmaker, measured Mrs Ryder for a frock for a wedding.

'You heard the latest, I suppose,' said Mrs Ryder out of the side of her mouth.

'No. What's that?'

'Spaghetti.'

'What about her?'

'Off again.'

'She's not.'

'She is.'

'My God.'

'Three months gone.'

'God love her.'

'Yeah but for how long? That's what I'd like to know. Will she manage to hang on to it this time?'

'Maybe, but then again ...'

'Yeah. Pigs might fly. Honest to God, the other night, nearly had a canary, thought the whole house was going to come in on top of us.'

'Go 'way?'

'Gone beyond the beyonds altogether he is. It'll be murder one of these nights, blue murder, see if it won't.'

'A terrible temper.'

'But she provokes him, Mrs D.'

'Is that a fact?'

'Well, the Ey-ties, you know yourself. Hot-blooded as hell.'

'Can't help feeling sorry for her all the same, the poor woman.'

'Who, Mammy?' Four eyes goggled as if I was a fish that had landed at their feet. 'What poor woman?'

'Little pitchers, Mrs D.' Mrs Ryder pulled her ear.

'You go on out and play now,' said Mammy.

'But—'

'Don't argue. Just do as you're told. And take D.J. with you; he could do with an airing.'

A few days later, Mrs Flynn had a black eye. She tried to hide it with her hand. When I asked her what had happened, she said she had walked into a door. But I didn't believe her.

The dining-room was freezing because the window was broken. A piece of cardboard was taped over the hole but it didn't fit, so the wind came through with a piercing whistle. Danny was sitting there shivering, but hot and red too as though with a fever. He didn't seem pleased to see me and became so wild killing the monster that I went home quickly without cocoa.

One night I was allowed to watch Mammy and Daddy getting ready for the Christmas dress-dance in the Metropole Ballroom. Mammy looked so glamorous and unfamiliar with her 'Which Twin

Has the Toni?' home-perm, scarlet nail-polish even on her *toes*, and the black on her eyes, that I felt shy. She had made the frock herself with eight yards of midnight-blue satin from McBirney's, at five-and-eleven a yard. It was beautiful. It stayed up by itself with bones, and swirled out at the bottom like a mermaid's tail. Her shoulders were bare and looked as white and soft as the rabbit-fur cape that I had around mine.

Daddy was Fred Astaire with his dicky-bow, the suit and the patent leather shoes. He had given Mammy a flower in a box that she called a 'corsage' and was pinning it to her front.

'Mind the boozalums, lamb.'

'Ah, the bountiful boozalums,' he said, kissing her shoulder.

She glanced at me in the mirror '*We* are not amused,' she murmured, flicking Daddy with her arm-length kid gloves.

He winked. 'She'll be the belle of the ball, won't she, Eily?'

'Yes.'

She flung a white silk scarf around his neck and he went downstairs singing about dancing with the same fortunate man.

Mammy perfumed a wad of cotton wool and pushed it between her boozalums. She held up the tiny dark-blue bottle. '"Sore de Paree". That's French, Eily. For "Evening in Paris".'

She buttoned her gloves, smiled into the mirror, then twirled around.

'Well, what do you think?'

'Could we get the police for Mr Flynn?'

'*What?*'

'The police cos he's always doing Mrs Flynn in and it's not fair because she's only a woman.'

'Good Christ!'

'And she's sick, I think, too, and has a black eye.'

Mammy took the cape from my shoulders and put it around her own. 'Amn't I always telling you not to be such a little Nosey Parker? Amn't I? Amn't I, Eily?'

'Yes.'

'Well how many times have I to tell you? Mind your own business, and I'll mind mine. Kiss your own sweetheart, and I'll kiss mine.'

'I know but—'

'No buts about it. What people do in their own houses is nobody's business but their own. You shouldn't even be thinking things like that, let alone saying them. Go on into bed now like a good girl, say your prayers and I'll get Granny to bring up a mugga cocoa and two bickies. Wouldn't that be nice?'

They each won a spot prize that night, Mammy a pound of tea for being the first one up with a ladder in her stocking and Daddy whiskey for knowing that Rodgers wrote the music, and Hart the words, of 'I Could Write a Book'.

'Danny was out at the crack this morning,' said Daddy a few days later. 'I was going to work, still dark it was. If this goes on, we'll have to reset our clocks.'

He smiled at me. But I looked into the fire and all I saw was Mr Flynn bashing up his wife. At night I heard her cries. Was it in dreams?

Then her lip was split and her left eye just a black slit in purple puffed-up flesh. I said nothing, although I couldn't help gasping. She didn't try to hide it.

Danny wasn't in the dining-room. I waited for a minute, then went to the kitchen door. Mrs Flynn was standing at the window with her back to me, looking out into the wintry garden.

'He's not there,' I said.

She said nothing.

'Why? Is he sick?'

'No.'

She spoke so quietly that I hardly heard, then heard myself speaking quietly too.

'Where is he?'

'He's … he's out.'

'But why? It's not his time.' Then I saw the ice-cream-maker on the floor in the corner, smashed into smithereens. 'Oh, Mrs Flynn! What happened?'

'I don't know, cara mia. I … don't know.'

Her shoulders were shaking, her voice breaking and I knew she was going to cry, so I ran out to get Danny and find out what was what.

He was way up at the very top of the road, where he never went. I ran beside him. He ignored me. I grabbed hold of him.

'Runnin' after your fella?' yelled Itchy.

'You'll never get him that way,' howled Gracie Fox.

I didn't care about them.

'Why are you out, Danny, why? It's not your time. Tell. Don't pretend you don't know me. You do. I tell you stories. Why, Danny? Why?'

It was like talking to the wall. But I didn't give up. I poked and pestered, trying to trip him up, to make him fall and force him to look and know me and talk. But I was wasting my breath. He was the train.

The winter got harder. Soon Danny was out at any old time, white streamers of frosty breath flowing out behind him, his face blue and yellow with the cold. Everyone noticed. No one said anything.

Then he stopped listening to my stories, wouldn't see me on the road. I pretended not to care and I kept calling to see if Mrs Flynn was alright, if she needed messages or anything. She always said she was fine thanks, Eily. But didn't look it.

One day a week before Christmas the wireless said it would snow, and at five o'clock it did: big fat flakes from a leaden yellow sky. And the snow stuck. By the time our tea was over, everything outside was covered in a soft white blanket. It looked nearly too beautiful to walk on.

We were allowed out until eight o'clock, snowball-fighting,

making snowmen and playing with the dogs, who raced around barking excitedly at every falling snowflake. Then, faces and fingers tingling, we thawed out by the fire with hot-buttered toast and mugs of cocoa.

Later, in bed, after Mousey and the big boys had gone home, it got as quiet as anything, the way it always does in snow. I put my book down, turned off my torch and snuggled into the fug, hoping that it would be too deep tomorrow for Eamonn, the baker's horse, to make it up the road so as I could go around with the baker's basket, taking orders from the women for small pans, large pans, milk pans, cottage pans, well-baked loaves, turnovers, crusty Vienna rolls ….

I woke up cold in pitch-black night, my heart hammering. I closed my eyes and listened hard. In the distance a dog. Others answered. Stopped. Then nothing, just deep, cottony quiet. But something had awakened me. Pulling the bedclothes around me for heat, I snaked to the end of my bed and looked out the window.

The snow had stopped. A fresh fall had smoothed the churned-up mess as a hot iron smooths a white sheet. It was perfect again, crisp and clean, with no people to ruin it. Our snowmen stood, chubbier and humpier now, blurry at the edges, calmly in control. In the pool cast by the street-light, the snow sparkled a pure, pale gold. Everyone seemed to be asleep.

Then I noticed the light in Flynn's hallway and the trail of ploughed-up snow that led away from the house up the road. And suddenly, there was Danny going hell-for-leather through the snow as though pursued by the Hound of the Baskervilles. In his pyjamas. Bare feet.

A scream that went on forever. Mrs Flynn stumbled out, collapsed into the snow, and began dragging herself away from the house, leaving a trail of pink.

Lights switched on; doors were opening.

I raced in to get Daddy. And then out to see.

Mrs Flynn was destroyed. Someone had bashed and smashed her until she was like a broken Christmas doll. Her face was a ruin. Blood trickled slowly from one ear. Making a deep dark hole in the snow.

Neighbours stood around, still and silent. Then Mrs Carr arrived with blankets and took over with her bossy English voice. Having been in the War she knew what to do: she covered Mrs Flynn with a blanket, ordered Mousey to fly to the Protestants' telephone for the ambulance.

It started snowing again. They made a tent over Mrs Flynn. Her eyes opened. We looked at each other. Then Mrs Carr grabbed me and said this was no place for children.

I walked around. It was like being in a dream. The women were strange and quiet, with greasy cold-cream faces and frightened eyes, some with curlers in, pipe-cleaners mostly, half-hidden by head-scarves, coats flung on over nighties and huge fur boots. The men were different too, pale and sombre. Dogs raced around barking like fools. Some kids started throwing snowballs.

Daddy and Mr Ryder suddenly appeared out of Flynn's house. Mr Ryder leaned into his hedge and got sick. Daddy sank into the snow and sat there with his face in his hands. The women ran over. Then: 'Jesus, oh Jesus,' clutching at one another, lighting desperate cigarettes.

'I knew this would happen. I knew it as God is my judge. I said it, oh Jesus!' said Mrs Ryder.

All talking at once. 'She had no choice.' 'He drove her to it.' 'Bound to happen.' 'Only a question of time.'

'God help her, the poor woman,' said Mammy.

The ambulance stopped at the bottom of the road and had to go into reverse because the road was narrow. People rushed to guide it up. I took advantage of the distraction to run into Flynn's house to see for myself.

Mr Flynn was sprawled out on the dining-room floor in the shape of a crucifix. One side of his head was caved in like an empty eggshell. The poker lay near his body. If it wasn't for all the blood, he could've been just drunk again.

When I came out of the house, many of the people had gone back to bed. There was nothing more to be done. And anyway, the wind was a blast of ice and the snow had turned sleety.

I tramped up the road for Danny, half-blinded, my face stinging. If I was cold, he was frozen. He stood there, a wet snowman with loose chattering teeth, not even pretending to let off steam. His face was purple. But I didn't care, took hold of his sleeve.

'You did it, didn't you?' I shouted above the wind.

He pulled his arm away. But I kept going. 'You did, didn't you? I know you did. Tell me, Danny. I don't care.'

He pulled away, pushed me and took off, crossing the road, down the other side. I caught up, stuck like glue. He was staring straight ahead, peering through the sleet that was clogging his eyelashes.

'I don't care,' I kept shouting. 'All I want to know is why, Danny. Why?'

Down the road I saw dark shapes move towards the yellow light from the back of the ambulance. Then the light went out. Danny stopped, gave a cry of despair. 'Mamma!'

I held onto him. 'I'm your friend, Danny. I told you stories. Tell me. It's only fair.'

He turned and looked at me. His face shone with wetness. 'The … monster must … die,' he said.

I nodded.

Danny caught up with the ambulance and ran behind it, a slight red figure in the tail-lights.

THE BLACK WIDOW

was stuffing lavender-bags for the Legion of Mary when Mrs
Kinch asked me to kindly call her Hettie, short for Henrietta,
since she was sick of Kinch and all it stood for.

Hettie? What could I say? I knew I could never call anyone
Hettie straight to their face without laughing, especially Mrs Kinch,
even if she was as gummy as Gabby Hayes, and had the long, bendy
neck of an ostrich.

And anyway, she was already called 'The Black Widow'.

Mrs Kinch lived with a smelly Scottie named Charlie on the
other side of Itchy Ryder. Although not exactly old, she always wore
clothes that were grimmer than my Granny's in winter. All black:
her frock, coat, cardigan and scarf, her small hat like the Pope's with
a nest of net, her gloves, shoes and stockings, shopping-bag and
umbrella. Her knickers were black too, Itchy had seen them on the
line and swore to it, big flapping bloomers, right down to your
knees.

So 'Black' made sense, but Mrs Kinch was no more a widow than
the man in the moon. She had monthly Masses said in Saint Mary's
for the repose of Mr Kinch's soul, but everyone knew that he was
living out in Inchicore with a fast Argentinian tango-dancer.

He had gone in the winter, on a Saturday evening. By Sunday,
Blarney Park was buzzing: *Didja hear? What d'you think? Isn't it desperate? Only cowped she is, Mrs K., God love her. Missed Mass this*

mornin', that'll tell you. And to look at him you'd think butter wouldn't melt. Oh. Some tango-dancer. So-called. You know yourself. Fast bitta goods. From Ar-gen-tina. Enough said. A cool customer Kinch alright, I twigged him long ago. And I wouldn't mind only it was outa the blue. 'That's it,' says he, in the middle of the tea. 'I've had enough.' God love her, she thought it was the sausages. And waltzes off in, I saw it waiting, Lawlor's taxi-cab. To Inchicore no less. All dickied out with his attaché-case, Eggsavier Cugat records and Captain Flint, of course, covered up in his cage. Look, here's one of his feathers. A nice green, isn't it?

I raced in with the news to my Ma and Da, who were papering the sitting-room. They got a fright in case I was a neighbour, or worse, a priest, because it was Sunday and a sin to do unnecessary, servile work. When I told them, they just lit cigarettes and stood there, saying nothing, mouths open like goldfish.

Mammy's head looked small in a green bandanna. Dried paste made Daddy's hair stand in spikes.

I tried again, slowly, in my best elocution: 'Mr. Kinch. Is. After. Running. Away.'

They frowned, blinking as if blinded by lights.

'From Mrs Kinch.'

Not a muscle moved, not a nostril, or even an eyelash. Smoke spiralled from their paste-frosted fingers.

'To Inchicore!' I shouted.

That did it: Mammy grabbed a stick, plunged it into the paste-pot and stirred the porridgy goo with great ferocity; Daddy turned with a pin to the paper to pop squashy bumps. 'A galloping horse'll never notice,' he muttered, wiping away oozy pearls with a rag that left streaks.

'Hm!' Mammy stood back, wiped her hands on her front and folded her arms like a shelf under her chest. 'Of course I'm not surprised,' she announced, to Daddy's back. 'Not one bit. We all know, don't we, that in the heel of the hunt, the nature of the beast never changes.'

Daddy's shoulders stiffened. He stopped wiping and stood as still as old Devlin's donkey on Dollymount Strand.

'What beast?' I asked.

'Unfortunately,' said Mammy.

There was a tight little silence, as if we were all waiting for a balloon to burst or Frankenstein's monster to walk in. Then Daddy turned around and looked at Mammy with sorry eyes. He stretched his hand with the rag in it towards her.

'And the sooner you learn that, the better,' she snapped at me.

'Learn what?'

'That men—'

'Don't, love,' said Daddy. 'Don't—'

'All men, even the best of them, are not to be trusted.' She flashed him a smile. 'That right, dear?'

Daddy heaved a sigh and closed his eyes as if he had a pain. With his long, sad face and spiky hair he was like a painting of Jesus with the Crown of Thorns, but with no beard or blood.

'Especially,' continued Mammy, 'when it comes to a bit of skirt.'

'How d'you mean, Mammy, skirt?'

'Christ Almighty!' roared Daddy, flinging away the rag. 'Is there to be no bloody end to it?'

'End? I'll give you end!'

She grabbed the paste-pot. He left the room. I sat on a chair.

I asked about the skirt again, after a minute, but Mammy just kept gazing into the paste-pot as if she had lost something in it, so I went out to play.

★

Summer meant the smell of camphor when, every May Day, whatever the weather, I went to Granny's where we opened the long wooden chest in her room, lifted out her pale summer clothes, and hung them up to air. After giving her dark winter things a good, stiff brushing, we folded them in tissue and laid them to rest among the rolling moth-balls. But summer seemed all the one to Mrs Kinch, who, still stuck in pitch, was Mammy's idea of a well-turned-out woman, very refined in her black, very ala mud. When I agreed that it was handy for not showing dirt, Mammy sighed like a mortified saint.

According to Mrs Kinch, Charlie had been tried and tested on life's fiery anvil and not found wanting, was the next best thing to a husband and, unlike one in particular—no names no pack-drill—was fidelity personified. That was all very well, but Charlie stank and his stink was the worst thing about him, worse than his temper, his scabby bald patches and his tongue which swelled up every day after his dinner and bulged out like raw liver until tea-time. How anyone could bear to nuzzle and pet him like Mrs Kinch did without get-ting sick was a mystery to me.

'That's love,' explained Mammy. 'True love. One of the signs. When you don't get the smell. Or if you do, don't mind. You get used to it. That's the thing about love, Eily. You put up with the pain.'

Mrs Kinch's back garden was full of lavender, all kinds of laven-der, from hazy blues to deep purples, roundy shrubs to tall spikes. You got it a mile off on a summer's day, a sunny, blue smell, like the soap Granny had for baths, big soap, too big to hold, mauve, beau-tiful. After a bath in Granny's I always felt so clean and cheerful that I wanted to sing and dance down the street the way they do in the pictures, but I never did in case people thought I was mad. They said 'The Whistler', downtown, was mad, and he didn't even dance, just stopped to whistle or sing a loud bit of opera at you. He did it to me once, in O'Connell Street, kneeling down on one knee, 'Laugh, Pagli-ahh-chi!' he bawled, tears rolling down his purple face, nearly making me cry too. People gave him wide berths and dirty looks. I thought he should've been on in The Royal, but he walked off before I could tell him. Up in Grangegorman, said everyone else. He's as mad as a clatter of hatters!

And maybe he was because he smelled worse than Charlie. So it wasn't soap that made him whistle and sing.

To get me out of the way every afternoon for two weeks, Mammy arranged that I should help Mrs Kinch with lavender-bags for the Legion of Mary sale of work. I didn't mind. I liked the smell and anyway I would be paid a shilling. The only problem was Charlie; just thinking about him made me sick, never mind having to smell him. After giving it some thought, Mammy came up with an idea that was a lie: over tea one day among the lavender, having told me to keep quiet, she informed Mrs Kinch that as a consequence of having been *savagely* bitten, when a mere child, by a *vicious* Kerry Blue, I was now terrified of all dogs.

'Poor little lambkin,' cried Mrs Kinch, with a face like Our Lady of Sorrows. 'Poor little mouse.'

'Ahem!' Mammy coughed with a warning glint to stop me from laughing.

Mrs Kinch gave me the last Iced Queen Cake and said the usual things—her dog was as gentle as a kitten, wouldn't hurt a fly—but, out of consideration, that she would confine him to his kennel whenever I was there. The kennel was away down at the bottom of the garden. Mammy smiled her satisfaction, slipped me a wink and passed her cup.

More tea was poured, milked, sugared, stirred. Mrs Kinch offered a plate of USA Assortment. 'And may I ask who owned it?'

'Owned what?' asked Mammy, choosing a Boudoir.

'The dog.'

'What dog?'

'The dog. The Kerry Blue. The one that attacked her.'

'Oh, *that* dog!' said Mammy (as if fifty had been discussed). She examined her Boudoir as though trying to add up a hard sum in her head, then her eyes lit up and she waved the biscuit around. 'Oh, years ago, Mrs Kinch, you wouldn't know them, it was … on a holiday.

Down the country. Yes, a farmer's dog, that was it, in Wexford. One June. The weather was lovely, well, not lovely exactly, we had rain of course, yes, plenty, but it wasn't a wetting rain, if you know what I mean, and never all day. If it rained in the morning, it stopped in the evening, thank God, and vice versa. Yes, in her calf, I'll never forget it, the left I think, was it? Or the right. Jumping off a haystack. There's something, I don't know, about Kerry Blues. You can't trust them.'

There were sighs and a sympathetic silence.

The back of my leg seemed to tingle with pain. It was in my calf. In the left or the right? Maybe there was a scar?

'And what part of Wexford was that?' asked Mrs Kinch. 'I'm from Ballynabola myself.'

'Jesus, the cake!' shrieked Mammy, jumping up. 'I've a Cut-and-Come-Again in the oven.'

If she had, I never got a bit of it.

I began to think about the Kerry Blue lies because my catechism said that no lie can be lawful or innocent and no motive, however good, can excuse a lie because a lie is always sinful and bad in itself.

'Ah, you don't have to take things so literally,' said Mammy. 'There are all kinds of lies. Black and white, and white don't count. White are only fibs.'

It said nothing about fibs in my catechism.

★

My job was easy: packing dried lavender into the little sachets which Mrs Kinch then sewed. The hard part was having to hear non-stop talk about the sweetness of Count John McCormack's tenor voice; the cunning of that damned elusive Pimpernel, de Valera; the splendour of the Eucharistic Congress in 1932; the mayhem in the North Strand when those jackbooted Germans bombed us to infinity; and wanting to be a nun when she was young in Ballynabola.

'It was all I ever wanted,' Mrs Kinch sighed. 'To be a bride of

Christ. To love and serve was all.'

'And why didn't you be?'

'Oh, I was. For a while, a postulant, but then … my health you see, my chest, it let me down.'

I looked at her chest, as flat and black as a canal. She patted it, breathed in and out; it hardly moved.

'What's apostulant?'

'A learner. But they didn't want me, couldn't use me. I was a burden, you see, because of my health. Of no account.'

Once, after making me say a perfect act of contrition, she brought me upstairs to the bare box-room and put me kneeling beside her by the narrow white bed. On one wall there was a big, silver crucifix, and on another, a dirty square rag with squiggles and fraying edges. It seemed a strange thing to want to have on a wall and I was going to ask her why it was there when she pointed at it in a holy manner with her chin.

'See that?'

'Yes.'

'Do you know what it is, pet?'

'No, what?'

She blessed herself quickly three times, then looked around as though expecting robbers. 'The shroud, the holy shroud,' she hissed. 'In the name of God, say nothing to no one.'

'Okay,' I hissed back, wondering why we were hissing.

'Not a word to a soul.'

'No.'

'Least said, soonest mended.'

'Okay.'

'Promise me now, pet.'

'I promise.'

'Good girl.'

We looked at each other in the silence that followed. She smiled and I knew that I liked her, with her eyes like hazelnuts, sweet lavender smell and pale, empty gums.

Then she ripped the covers off the bed, saying she was going to teach me something that she had learned long ago in the convent, something that was useful and practical but, at the same time, enriching. This turned out to be the Art of Proper Bedmaking, which meant that the big hem goes at the top and the small at the bottom. I understood then why there were two different-sized hems on a sheet. (Mammy laughed and said Mrs Kinch was better value than Jimmy O'Dea.)

After the bed was made according to the Proper Art, we sat on it and Mrs Kinch advised me on no account to ever let my brothers or any boy into the bed with me.

'Why not?'

'Because boys will be boys; they … do things to you.'

'I know. They puck you. Look.' I showed my bruise where Andy had bashed me, but she didn't look.

'No, pet, no. Not that. Other things. Bold, dirty things.'

'Like what?'

She preferred not to say; it was probably sticking tongues together because Mammy had told us that that was *very* bold (even though it only tickled) and if she ever caught us again she'd skin us alive.

Sometimes for a change from talking, Mrs Kinch read aloud from Catholic Truth Society pamphlets that she bought in the church for thruppence. They were usually boring, sometimes interesting, and always about sins of the flesh.

I began to wonder and think.

'It's under your skin, isn't it?' I asked one day in the middle of 'Chastity'.

'What?'

'Your flesh.'

'Of course.'

'Between your skin and your bones?'

'I should hope so. Where else would it be in the name of God?' She laughed softly, covering her mouth with her hands.

'Well then. How could it suddenly burst out by itself and, say … take the name of the Lord thy God in vain?'

'What?'

'Or not keep holy the Sabbath day?'

'What?'

'Or not honour thy father and thy mother or covet thy neighbour's wife? That's what I'd like to know.'

Mrs Kinch looked at me with her head so far over that it nearly tipped her shoulder.

'The thing is,' I said. 'You'd have to think of it first, of the sin, wouldn't you? Of doing it. Your flesh couldn't pop out and do it by itself, could it? Rob or kill? So the sins of the flesh should really be sins of the head.'

Mrs Kinch thought for a while and then declared to God that I was either a proper little Pagan or a Jesuit; didn't know which was worse, but that she would pray for me anyhow.

Then one morning Charlie was found in his kennel, as dead as a doornail. Mrs Kinch was sad but not surprised. Pining, she said he was. 'For Captain Flint. Not to mention the other, no names no pack-drill. Boon companions they were, from the beginning. Boon companions.' Her face twitched, her eyes were red, her hankie was wet.

I felt sorry for not liking Charlie.

My Da came over and dug the grave and Charlie, wrapped in old newspapers, was buried quietly. The kennel was burnt (the street stank for days) except for two bits of wood which were saved for a cross.

Mrs Kinch spoke about Charlie as a pup, the mischief he had got up to, the things he had chewed to mush. She decided to plant a rosemary bush, when subsidence had ceased, since rosemary was for remembrance.

One day, at the end of the two weeks, Mrs Kinch packed some Lipton tea, Jeyes Fluid, pamphlets, and rat poison into her shopping-bag and told me we were off on a corporal work of mercy to Marshalsea Barracks. I was delighted.

We got the bus to Nelson's Pillar and walked up along Aston Quay, past McBirney's big store. The Liffey looked dangerous, dark and choppy, although the day was bright and calm. A navy-blue Guinness barge ploughed low through the water, weighed down with its barrels of stout. As it approached Richmond Bridge, its funnels folded down and under it went, safe and sound. There was a man on the deck. I waved to him and he waved to me. He was wearing a navy-blue jumper.

A strong sickly-sweet smell filled the air. Mrs Kinch sniffed it and made a face. 'God love him all the same though.'

'Who?'

'Poor Father Mathew. When you think of it. A blessed saint and martyr like that having to live with the ruination of the city he gave his life for, being brewed under his very nose.'

'Oh.' (I frequently didn't know what Mrs Kinch was talking about.)

We turned away from the quays, she droning on, like a bee in my ear, about poor Father Mathew and the demon drink. I stopped listening.

When we turned in to the place that was the Marshalsea Barracks, my heart began to feel anxious. I had been expecting a square yardful of spick-and-span soldiers, marching, all in the right step, to bright bugle bands, in high, shiny boots. But this was nothing like that. This Marshalsea Barracks was a terrible place: all battered, bleak and falling down, with barred and broken windows, more like a prison than a place for people to live in, and with a smell that was worse than Charlie's, the brewery's, and the Whistler's all mingled together.

A boy crouched near a big, dark, open doorway, playing with the pedal of a Gas-man's yellow bike. He was barefoot and filthy. His clothes were rags; you could see his bones poking through. He was the poorest boy I had ever seen. A tiny tattered girl of about three sat whimpering on the ground, like a sad little monkey, scratching with both hands at her head of matted hair. I wanted to give her a bath in Granny's and sweet Goody after in a cup. A raucous woman barged bawling from the barracks in a black shawl with a baby tucked into it. You would've heard her up in the Phoenix Park if you were deaf in both ears. 'Jaysus' was the only word I recognised. Mrs Kinch blessed herself three times. The boy cowered behind the bike. The little girl was whacked and yanked off, yelling.

It was as though she was being hauled into hell.

'Where are the soldiers?' I asked.

'What soldiers? Oh, the soldiers, no. Only the poor live here now. The very poor. It's years since there were soldiers.'

My heart sank even further. I didn't want to be there. Then I remembered God saying that the poor were blessed and would get into heaven first, so that cheered me up.

Mrs Kinch stopped just outside the big front door to fish in her pocket. She came up with a lavender-bag. 'Here, pet. Stick your nose into that and you'll come to no harm.'

I had just taken it from her black-gloved fingers when a shower of sick, followed by a white-faced young man, shot through the doorway, missing us by inches. He leaned with one hand against the wall, heaving. His leather money-bag hit the ground. Pennies rolled. I ran to pick them up and so did the poor boy.

The young man apologised while cleaning himself with a spotless hankie. Mrs Kinch assured him that she was untouched and it could happen to a bishop. He doubted whether any bishop had ever had the temerity to put as much as a toe into such a hell-hole.

'Oh, come, come,' said Mrs Kinch. 'We'd be lost without our shepherds.'

He was the Gas-man, owner of the bike, a coin-meter collector, with a handsome face, blonde hair and thick eyelashes. (He had missed a bit of sick on his tie but I didn't like to say so.)

'My first time here. I knew it was bad; I was warned but wasn't expecting …' he shuddered, blowing out air.

'You'll get used to it.'

'I doubt it.'

'Oh, you will of course, with the help of God.'

'God?' His pleasant face changed. He turned to look back through the open door. 'What God?'

'Now, now! None of that, if you please,' snapped Mrs Kinch.

When the pennies were picked up, the Gas-man took a three-penny-bit from his pocket and gave it to the boy, who just stood there gawking at it, as if he didn't know what it was. 'Go on,' said the Gas-man, 'buy something for yourself. An ice-cream, or a Lucky Lump.'

'Thanks, Mister,' said the boy in a hoarse voice, scuttling off in high glee.

I thought I should get something too because fair is fair and I had picked up just as many, but I didn't, so was I secretly glad about the sick on his tie.

The Gas-man put on his bicycle-clips, tied his money-bag over the crossbar and got up on his bike.

'Bye-bye now,' said Mrs Kinch. 'God bless.'

'I mean no disrespect, Ma'am,' he said quietly, 'but if there is a God, then he's an effing sadist.'

'See that?' said Mrs Kinch, looking after him. 'A Communist. It's the likes of him and his ilk that has the world in the state it's in today.'

She clamped the lavender-bag to my nose, took my hand and

marched me into the barracks, down a freezing, dark, stone passage lined with heavy wooden doors that had spy-holes in them. Snatches of noise rose and fell as we hurried past: arguments, shouts, smashes, laughs, cries, clangs, barks, a man singing 'I Dreamt I Dwelt in Marble Halls'. Smells came seeping through the lavender; awful smells, of piss, pig-swill and cats. Broken light bulbs were swathed in cobwebs as thick as my arm and blacker than Mrs Kinch's coat. Mushrooms, like evil warts, sprouted from the walls.

At the end of the passage Mrs Kinch stopped and hammered on a door. Her face was grim. My heart thumped. My skin was clammy. I tried to stop breathing. The door was eventually dragged open by a dwarf-like dirty little man. His smell hit my stomach hard. I tore away from Mrs Kinch and ran out of the barracks at top speed.

Mrs Kinch wasn't long. All she had done was say the Legion prayers, make tea, and put down rat poison.

'You were quite right to leave, if that was the way you felt,' she said, as we walked off. 'You should always obey your instincts. Which is what I'm going to do now, come hell or high water.'

Then she stopped talking. (I asked was there something wrong but she said there wasn't.) We got on and off another bus and hurried to a small house on a pavement with dusty windows and no front garden. Mrs Kinch straightened her back, knocked and blessed herself three times. A cheerful smiling woman, with red lipstick, green high-heels, jet-black hair, brown eyes, and a big chest like Jane Russell's, in a stripey blue-and-yellow frock, opened the door.

'Good afternoon,' said Mrs Kinch, in a high quick voice. 'Excuse the intrusion, but perhaps you'll agree, when you know who I am, that it's time we met. My maiden-name is Funge, Henrietta Funge, late of Ballynabola, County Wexford. I believe you're acquainted with one Benjamin, better known as Benny Kinch. My husband.'

The woman was astonished. She held on to the door. Her smiling red mouth fell open. She looked from me to Mrs Kinch, then back to me again. Her eyes widened. 'Jesus!' she gasped. Her knees buckled and her hands, with their nail-polish, slid down the doorjamb into a real slow faint.

The hall was very narrow but we managed to drag her down it. Somewhere Captain Flint was reciting his poem. 'Hold off, unhand me, grey-beard loon,' he squawked.

'Ah, God love him,' sighed Mrs Kinch. 'He's still at it.'

She flung a cup of water over the woman who, recovering, immediately asked for the love of God if Mrs Kinch did nothin' else would she please take that bloody parrot with her when she was goin', because it had her driven up the walls with the poetry.

Mrs Kinch blinked. 'For an Argentinian,' she said stiffly, 'you have a very Dublin accent.'

'A what? Listen! I don't know who you've been talkin' to, but I'm a Boggins, love. Betty. From Ballybough. And you can't get more Dublin than that.' There was a silence. 'Argentinian my foot! Listen, come here till I tell you. The number eight tram to Booterstown, when the tide was out, is as far as ever I got.'

She had the kind of laugh that made you laugh too. Even Mrs Kinch smiled.

Betty Boggins looked down at me, her eyes clouded with concern. She put her hand on Mrs Kinch's black sleeve. 'I swear to God, I didn't know … I had no idea … is this …?'

'No,' said Mrs Kinch.

'Oh.'

'We weren't blessed with any.'

'Ah.'

'And anyway I never went in for that kind of caper.'

'No,' said Betty Boggins, cheering up. 'Ah well sure, it takes all sorts to make a world, doesn't it?'

'It does,' agreed Mrs Kinch. 'And it'd be a dull existence if we were all the same.'

'Well, honest to God, you could sing that if you had an air to it. Now tell us, I'm sure youse could do with a nice cuppa tea.'

Women always make tea to talk, and they talked and talked. I got fed up and so, when the biscuits were all gone, I went off to listen to Captain Flint, who had got as far as 'With my cross-bow I shot the albatross.'

★

A week later Mr Kinch came back to Mrs Kinch the same way that he had gone, in Lawlor's taxi-cab. He got a great welcome from Blarney Park. Everyone thought he looked fatter and more contented.

Daddy said that change is sometimes necessary, but that home is where the heart is. He looked at Mammy when he said that and she smiled as if she had got a birthday present.

The following week who should arrive in Lawlor's taxi-cab, all business, but Betty Boggins, with a big trunk, a bicycle, a small palm tree, a box of delph, a gilt mirror, and two cases of records.

Blarney Park buzzed again: *Lodger my hat! Talk about havin' your cake and eatin' it! Worse than Mohammedans. Nice work if you can get it, heh-heh-heh! A disgrace that's what it is, in a Catholic country, a bloody disgrace.*

But it didn't last long because life went back to normal: Mr Kinch trotted off to the bank as usual every morning with his line of pens in his pocket; he cleaned the windows, put out the dustbin, cut the grass, gave free advice about money to those who needed it and won a Silver Cup in the Blarney Park tennis tournament. Mrs Kinch went to Mass, did the messages, washing, ironing and got the dinners. (The monthly Masses were cancelled.) The only difference now was that every evening Betty Boggins cycled off to her job at the Morosini-Whelan School of Dancing.

Many's the sunny afternoon Itchy and I sat on the back wall while Mrs Kinch, her long neck snapping, tangoed with passion through the lavender, to Eggsavier Cugat. She looked so happy and seemed to have found her true vocation at last, in the colourful arms of Betty Boggins, the fast Argentinian tango-dancer from Ballybough.

THE REAL
ALL-IRELAND BEAUTY

When the competition for The All-Ireland Beauty was announced on the wireless, with a Hollywood screen-test as part of the prize, I thought of Hope Fay. With her beautiful chestnut hair, red lips and big, green eyes, Hope was as nice as any film star, and *much* nicer than June Allyson.

Hope was an only girl who lived up the road with her father and mother. Her three brothers, Father Patrick, Father Brendan and Father Joseph, had all became priests together. On the day of their ordination, everyone (bar the Protestants) knelt down in a bunch to receive their first priestly blessing. It went on for ages and was worse than Mass: Mr Ryder fell asleep and keeled over; Nero, the egg-lady's dog, howled at every *Dominus vobiscum*; and, between the rain and holy water, we all got drenched. Then the priests ate their first priestly breakfast and went off to the Missions to convert Pagans with no clothes on into Catholics.

Hope's father was a retired science teacher called Alo the Crank whose real name was Aloysius. He was supposed to be a real clever Dick, but sitting at his front window, spitting and scowling out at everything that passed on two legs or four, didn't seem like the height of cleverality to me. I didn't like him; he wouldn't give the ball back when it went into his garden, always looked as if he had swallowed a lemon, and never stopped giving out about shouting. As if you could play without shouting.

Mammy thought Alo was the bee's knees. 'He's so distinguished-looking. So handsome and with such fine eyes. A cross between Frederic March and Melvyn Douglas. And I'd lay any bets that underneath that stern exterior there beats a heart of living flesh.'

'How d'you know?'

'What?'

'About the heart.'

'Oh. It's … those eyes … that little moustache. It's something I just feel in the marrow of my bones.'

My Ma's marrow told her about everything from the weather to the toughness of meat or the saltiness of bacon, whether people were decent and respectable like us or snobs with put-on accents. It warned her about the pictures too. 'Brutal,' she'd say, after a stab. 'But I knew it would be. Felt it in the marrow of my bones.'

One thing that Mammy couldn't fathom was what Alo the Crank had ever seen in his wife. 'A waitress in the Belvedere Hotel is all she was. A man with his education and appearance. Incomprehensible.'

'What does that mean?'

'And I wouldn't mind but she's plain as a pikestaff to boot and always was.'

'What's a pikestaff?'

'A fish.'

'A fish?'

'Yes, a fish.'

'What kind of a fish?'

'A canal fish. Like a perch, only worse. An awful, ugly-looking thing altogether.'

'Can you eat it?'

'Holy God! Fulla bones and with two rows of teeth? Would you want to?'

Once, a scrawny, one-eyed red hen skittered into my Cork Granny's kitchen tailed by the usual band of beaky attackers, all squawking and pecking. The commotion was fierce. Blood spurted. Feathers flew. Granny swished the broom, sweeping the big hens out. The little hen lay there, reminding me of the lamb I had seen whose eyes had been pecked out by crows.

'Is it dead? Did they kill it?'

'They did.'

'Why, Granny, why? Why were they after it?'

'Because she was the weak one, the imperfect one.'

'But that's not fair.'

'Not by our lights maybe no. But it's nature, Eily, nature. Red in toot'n claw. You can't lick nature.'

To me, Hope Fay's Ma, with her habit of rushing in bursts on thin, bandy legs, was more like that little hen than any fish I had ever eaten, seen in fishmongers, or the canal, or the sea. And if hens could speak, I was sure it would be in the same nervous way—as if afraid of a secret she might let out, by accident.

I got friendly with Hope from selling tickets door-to-door. 'Like to buy one?' I asked as, encased in a white face-pack, she peered out like a reluctant ghost.

'How much?' she asked, barely moving lips that were as red as the poppies in Hacker's Field.

'A penny each or a shilling the book. You get one for nothing.'

'What's it in aid of?'

'A monster raffle for the conversion of China.'

The face-mask crinkled. Her eyes gleamed like emeralds from deep snow.

'It's a good cause,' I said. 'China.'

She laughed. The mask cracked open. Puffs of white fell onto the blue neck of her blouse. 'Come on in till I see if I've any money.'

Mrs Fay was doing the kitchen tiles with a tin of Cardinal Red. She seemed smaller in her house than in the street. Her hair was dark red in a streely bun and her skin was transparent, like tissue, with two burny pink dots on her cheeks. She nodded at me in a worried way, then returned to the hard work of spreading the polish.

I followed Hope into the front room. Alo the Crank sat by his window, reading a thick book. 'What's this?' he barked, looking up. 'What's the meaning of this interruption?'

'Sorry, Pa, but I'm just buying a ticket,' murmured Hope, rooting in her handbag.

He grunted, then glared at me as if I was a maggot in an apple. Not that I cared.

I put on a smile, pretending to like him. 'Would you like to buy one too, Mr Fay? It's in aid of a good cause. The Holy Ghost Missions for the conversion of—'

'Pheh!'

He hoiked up a gollier and shot it, with good aim, into a chipped enamel jug on the floor beside his armchair. Then, staring hard at me, he took a handkerchief from his pocket and wiped his mouth with it.

What was up with him? Did he think I was going to rob an ornament off the mantelpiece or something? As if I'd be bothered!

I looked away from the cold grey eyes that Mammy thought were so fine. It was very quiet. Hope was scratching away, writing her name and address in my ticket-book. I looked at the wallpaper; faded flowers, too faded to see faces in. I looked up at the ceiling; it was as yellow as the one in my Cork Granny's kitchen, but without the cobwebs. I looked at his phlegm floating in the jug, shivering like runny pale-green sago. In my mind I saw the sign in the buses— Spitting Prohibited In or On the Bus. Forty Shilling Fine—and wanted to shout it into his face.

Then, as if reading my mind, he roared 'Waugh!' in a terrible voice. I nearly wet my knickers in fright and grabbed at Hope. She gave a pleasant smile and went back to her writing. Her hand wasn't even shaking.

Then the door opened and Mrs Fay came in, looking weary. She made straight for the jug, picked it up and walked out, closing the door gently behind her.

Alo the Crank smiled, a slow, cruel smile, and I could suddenly see what Mammy meant about Frederic March; but Frederic March gone wrong, if you ask me.

Hope worked in A. Alexander's Haberdasher's, between the Bank of Ireland and Madame Marcia's Hair Salon. It was a tiny shop, smelling of dust and the Russian cigarettes that A. Alexander smoked, and with a bell that tinkled every time the door opened. The walls were packed from floor to ceiling with boxes of buttons, braids, elastic, needles, threads, darning-wools, ribbons, hairnets, handkerchiefs, Bradmola nylons, Lisle stockings, Vedonière vests, ladies' knickers with double gussets, Fair Isle pullovers, snake-belts, Liberty bodices, men's long combinations and First Holy Communion gloves.

In May I was sent to buy three hankies for my Da's birthday. The bell tinkled and Hope looked up from her *Silver Screen* magazine.

'Well, if it isn't the little Chinese converter herself. How are you, Eily?'

Her smile was lovely; it made you feel happy, as if someone liked you and thought you were nice.

When I gave my order, she flipped her chair over into a ladder and climbed up it. Her legs were curvy and bright, in tan nylon stockings and black high heels. A red nail-polish blob stopped a snaky ladder in one stocking. The skin underneath it was white and freckled. One seam was dead straight and I was wondering should I tell her about the other when boxes came tumbling all over the place.

'Damn it anyway,' cursed Hope. 'And me only after racking them. Like to give us a hand?'

I loved being behind the counter; it was a different world, much better than playing shop with empty boxes and stuff, because it was a real shop. Once Hope even let me mind it while she flew into Madame Marcia's for five minutes with a nasty case of the runs.

Hope's boyfriend, Iggy French, was a tall, slouching fellow with bockety teeth and pimples, who worked in the bank. He came from someplace that he called the 'wettest boghole on mudder eart'. Sometimes it was hard to know what Iggy was saying, because, as well as the teeth, pimples and slouch, he had a very peculiar accent.

Hope said his slouch came from leaning over money all day that didn't belong to him. 'It's enough to give anyone the pip,' she laughed. 'Let alone the hump, d'you get it?'

I did, after a while, and then I laughed too.

Hope loved Bette Davis and wanted to be like her in every way possible, but she was too tall and her face was different, so all she could do was smoke like Bette Davis. She was a real star actress herself and kept me in fits with accents and 'Aye, aye, aye! I like you vairy mush', dancing, like Carmen Miranda, with piled-up boxes on her head instead of bananas. 'You should go in for the All-Ireland Beauty,' I said, and I wasn't just saying it. 'You could get into the pictures. You'd be good in Hollywood.'

'Well, maybe I will,' was all she said.

Every dinner-hour, Iggy swopped leaning over money to lean over A. Alexander's counter with the moony eyes of a sick cow. You could see how madly in love with Hope he was, even if you were blind, deaf and dumb in a fog on the top of Carrauntoohil. It was easy to see what he saw in Hope but what she saw in him was beyond me.

One sunny Sunday, they took me with them out on a jaunt. We queued for tram number eight, at Nelson's Pillar, right in the middle of O'Connell Street, and when it came we sat upstairs on the outside for the benefit of air. The tram was packed with happy people in summer hats and sandals. My stomach fluttered with joy as we trundled along through the salty, sleepy towns of Blackrock, with its swimming baths, and Dun Laoghaire, with its piers and promenade. When we reached the end of the line, at an old town called Dalkey, Iggy bought a bottle of lemonade from a crusty old man in a fusty old shop.

Iggy promised to return the bottle but the man still charged him tuppence on it. 'Oul skinflint,' muttered Iggy.

We climbed a furzy hill and when we got to the top, sweating, we found a grassy spot, near people and two monuments. It was lovely to lie there, like a dream, with the breeze in the trees, a buzz of bees, the birds, and distant laughter.

When you sat up, you saw the sea, a sheet of silver spangles, stretched between hazy mountains on one side and on the other the Hill of Howth.

We got hungry and ate our picnic, which was lovely, of a hard-boiled egg each with a twist of salt, jam sandwiches and an apple. There was cake as well which I had to spit out because of caraway seeds, but I did it politely, the way I was taught, into my hankie.

Iggy's manners were worse than the chimpanzees' tea-party; he grabbed without offering, scoffed, chomped, slurped, spoke with his mouth full, patted his belly and belched like a boy without as much as once begging our pardon.

He took Hope's left hand in his and I thought it was going to get romantic, but all he wanted to do was to pick his teeth with her little fingernail. She pulled her hand away and told him to use a matchstick like everyone else. He wasn't too pleased, so he slouched off with himself for a ramble.

Hope slipped off her sandals and turned over onto her stomach. Her skirt, the colour of crushed raspberries and cream, clung to her bottom, making it look like a round, soft summer jelly.

'I'd give anything to get away,' she sighed. 'To have a bash at life. Anything.'

'Try the All-Ireland,' I said. 'You might win. Your hair is lovely.'

'Iggy says it's so wavy it makes him seasick just to look at it.'

He came back in bad humour, waving his arms about. 'Know who's responsible for all a diss?' he demanded.

'All of what?' asked Hope.

'Diss. De park, stachas an' all.'

'Haven't a clue.'

'Bloody Queen Victoria.'

'Well, so what? Here, Ignatius,' she patted the grass, 'sit down and take the weight off your mind. You look as hot as a roasted goose.'

'Marry me wudja for de love of Jayz and not be drivin' me mad,' bawled Iggy.

'No, Iggy. I won't. Now let that be an end to it for once and for all.'

Relief flooded into me like water into a lock.

'Dat's dat den.' Iggy grabbed his belongings and set off down the hill.

'Would you look at him,' said Hope. 'The broken-hearted lover, moryah! But with the bottle under his oxter for the tuppence all the same. Skinflint!'

I had to stop myself from doing a jig for joy.

'Men are always on at you, Eily, for one thing or the other. Usually the other. Marry Iggy! And end up like my Mother? Ever at his beck and call? A fate worse than death.'

A few days later, when Hope decided to enter the the All-Ireland, Alo threatened to throw her out, saying the contest was a vulgar circus for men to leer lewdly at women. Her mother said nothing. Not that it would have made any difference; Hope's mind was set on winning and I was delighted. She got a Kelly green taffeta frock, wholesale, from A. Alexander, and had her photograph taken by Ross of Stephen's Green.

Looking beautiful in her Kelly green, Hope sailed through the heats to become the Leinster Beauty. Blarney Park was in heaven. Mammy's marrow told her Hope would win the final too, because Munster had hips like a heifer, Connacht's eyes were pissholes in snow, and Ulster's nose was too pointy.

Two days before the final, when excitement was intense and the betting ferocious, Mrs Fay coughed up so much blood that she was rushed by ambulance to Saint Mary's Chest Hospital in the Phoenix Park, where she died the next day.

On the day after that, Munster with the heifer hips became the All-Ireland Beauty.

Hope gave up A. Alexander's shop soon afterwards in order to care for her father. I went back to school and didn't see her for a while. At Christmas I got a present from my auntie of an art-silk hankie with the face of Bette Davis on it. It was awful, but I thought that Hope might like it, so I called up to see her.

Alo the Crank sneered at the hankie. But it wasn't for him any-way, was it? Hope liked it. She put it into a empty chocolate box, marked 'Treasured Memoranda', in which there were photographs of herself as the Leinster Beauty. We looked and admired them, me smiling, she sighing.

You were lovely, I wanted to tell her. You're the real All-Ireland Beauty.

Alo the Crank cleared his throat and spat, then banged on the floor. 'That needs emptying,' he said.

Hope closed her eyes. Then she bent down, picked up the jug and took it from the room, closing the door very gently behind her.

BELLEEK, PHILISTINES AND MISFITS

The music teacher, Mr Harold Savidge, B.A. Mus. Trinity College, lived up the road in 'Jodhpur', with his pale yellow sister, Miss Lillian, and a marmalade cat called Gervaise. They were old but not crotchety.

I started piano lessons and, although I wasn't any good, Mr Savidge never rapped me over the knuckles with a stick or pulled my hair, like other piano teachers were said to do. As a matter of fact, he always made me a cup of tea, 'Darjeeling, my dear, the champagne of teas,' after the lesson, and told me tales of life in Rajasthan where he and Miss Lillian had spent so many happy years.

They had had an academy there: The Savidge Academy of Musical and Terpsichorean Arts. He had photographs of shy Indian Princesses at grand pianos with himself standing by in a white suit, with his dark, droopy moustache and headful of young hair.

Miss Lillian was the Fancy Dancing and Deportment teacher; she was young and lovely in the photographs too, dancing in bare feet with flowing chiffon scarves. But then she had a riding accident. Her Dancing and Deportment days were over forever.

From the outside, except for strings of beads at the windows instead of curtains, 'Jodhpur' looked ordinary. But inside was like being in *The Arabian Nights* or a dream that smelled of sandalwood. There was no lino and the floorboards were polished to a sunny honey colour. In the hall a painted elephant held a brass gong which, when touched lightly with its chamois striker, made a mellow golden sound that meant that it was time for tea. Camphor- and cedar-wood boxes, ivory chess and backgammon sets, bead-encrusted pouches and strange pipes sat about on carved tables. Upstairs, one bedroom was a library with walls of books and worn leather armchairs on either side of the tiny black iron fireplace. Two photographs stood on the mantelpiece: one was of 'Applewood House' in County Meath, where the Savidges had grown up; the other was of Miss Lillian and 'Sunspright', a grey horse she had got for her fourteenth birthday.

They were very old photographs.

Downstairs, the folding doors between the dining- and sitting-rooms were always open. In the sitting-room (they called it the music-room), instead of the usual couch, armchairs, china cabinet, and small table, there was a huge mirror which reflected the piano, piano-stool, mahogany gramophone, and twelve green leather record-cases. An enormous heap of peacock-blue cushions were piled higgledy-piggledy in a corner. Sometimes after my lesson Mr Savidge shouted 'For this relief, much thanks,' diving into the blue like a slim electric fish. Then I'd sound the gong and Miss Lillian would come downstairs with one of the silk shawls she always wore around her twisted shoulders. Gervaise usually joined us since he was partial to his saucer of Darjeeling.

Mr Savidge's star pupil was a boy of fourteen, Georgie Sweeney, who lived up the road. Mammy told me that when he was nine, his Ma, having discovered that he had a great ear, bought Georgie a secondhand piano with the fifty-five pounds she had inherited from her mother, and sent Georgie to Mr Savidge for lessons. He was a natural. In no time at all he was in with the grown-ups at the Sunday musical evenings, accompanying them or playing 'The Robin's Return' and 'Für Elise' on the piano, without mistakes.

I remember Mrs Sweeney: a delicate, bright-eyed lady, quick and neat as a blackbird, whose song was 'I'll Take You Home Again,

Kathleen'. She sang it with her head flung back and hands prayfully pressed against the curving black front of her frock. A magnificent rendering, the men pronounced, swallowing stout while the small port and sweet sherry women smiled icily. And Georgie looked at his mother with love and pride.

Then, when he was twelve, Georgie came in from school one day and found her on the kitchen floor with her head in a galvanised bucket of dirty water. The scrubbing-brush was still clenched in one cold blue hand. Her heart had given out. She had fallen in.

Shortly after the funeral her older sister, Auntie Maureen from Galway, came to look after Georgie and his Da and cook their dinners for them. Auntie Maureen was a nurse with a brisk manner, who always wore her sleeves rolled up, even in the winter. Her arms were like a thin horse's legs.

Georgie's Da was a quiet-as-a-mouse man, who sold socks in Arnotts and could tell you anything you ever wanted to know about Roman viaducts, aqueducts, walls, roads and bridges. He sucked away on an empty pipe, having willingly given up tobacco years before because his beloved dead wife couldn't abide the stink.

My Ma expressed no surprise but wasn't at all pleased when, as soon as the year was up, Mr Sweeney got special permission from His Holiness, the Pope, removed his black tie and armband and quietly married the Auntie Maureen.

Not long afterwards we were drinking tea in 'Jodhpur' when Georgie arrived with a letter. He gave it to Mr Savidge and joined us at the table but wouldn't have tea. His eyes were red and the lashes were wet.

'Unbelieveable,' muttered Mr Savidge.

'What is, Harold?' asked Miss Lillian.

He waved the letter. 'She's, that is, Georgie's mother ... is selling his piano.'

'His piano?'

'Yes.'

They looked at Georgie. His eyes filled with tears.

'It seems …' continued Mr Savidge, his face getting pink, 'it appears that she is the proud possessor of … a china cabinet.'

'A china cabinet?' echoed Miss Lillian.

'Just so. Inherited. From her mother. And there's nowhere else to put it. Hah!' He walked around. 'There's nowhere else to put the damn thing so the piano has to go. A bloody china cabinet!'

'Yeah but it's full of Belleek.' They all looked at me as if I had two heads. 'My Ma says it's priceless.'

Georgie jumped up sobbing. 'I hate her I hate her and she's not my mother.' He ran out of the room and up the stairs.

Mr Savidge grabbed an orange from a bowl and began to tear the peel off it, muttering to himself.

'Now, Harold,' warned Miss Lillian.

'Good God!' Leaping to his feet, he marched around the room, appealing to the ceiling, the orange-peel flapping. 'And what about music? And talent? Nurturing God-given talent? What about that? Eh?'

Miss Lillian sighed and shook her head.

I didn't know what everyone was getting so excited about.

'What's Belleek?' I asked Mammy as she finecombed my hair that night.

'What's what?'

'In the Auntie Maureen's cabinet, Belleek. What is it?'

'H'm! Belleek how are ya. It's far from Belleek that one was reared, I can tell you, and her sister hardly cold, very far from Belleek, or anywhere else for that matter, oh, a smooth operator alright, the grave must be churnin', if you want to know me come and live with me, a smooth and slick operator alright for all her shenanigans and no mistake.'

'But what *is* it?'

'Oh hold still or I'll give you Belleek,' Mammy said, crushing a louse with her blood-spattered thumb-nail.

A few days later a man and two boys trundled up the road in a horse and cart. With much advice from the neighbours, they hoisted the piano onto the cart and trotted it off to the woman in Glasnevin who had bought it out of the *Evening Mail* for eighty pounds.

I saw Georgie slinking out of the house and followed him up the canal. He stood on the bank firing stones at birds.

'You'll kill one and then you'll be sorry,' I shouted.

He turned. 'Buzz off you. You're only a kid.'

A stone connected.

'Now look what you've done,' I screamed, as a small bird fell, its wings fluttering, and was swept over the lock down into the thundering blackness below.

'You eejit!' I punched him. 'You big eejit.'

He pushed me away, sat down on the bank, and, to my surprise, put his face into his hands and cried as if his heart was broken.

I felt sorry for him, but said nothing. Eventually he stopped crying.

'I didn't mean it, I swear.' He looked at me. His eyes were the silvery-grey of a clean pigeon's wing and his lashes as thick and damp as Greta Garbo's in *Camille*.

I sat down beside him. 'Ah well, it's only a bird,' I said by way of comfort. 'There's plenty more.'

Georgie started talking. He hated the Auntie Maureen; she smelled of the suet she chewed to keep the cold out, moaned in the night and forced him to eat tapioca every day although it made him vomit. Even his father, who had never shouted before, or used bad language, had yelled at him to 'eat the bloody frogspawn can't you, for the love of Christ, and get it over with!' But the worst thing was that she hated the piano. *That feckin' nise,* she said when he played it.

On the way back through Hacker's Field, we saw Mousey Heron and the big boys scouring the ditch for rats to torture and drown.

Georgie grabbed me. His face was white. 'Duck, Eily, duck!'

'Why? What's wrong?'

'Nothing. Hide. Don't let them see me, please.' He pulled me behind a bush.

'Okay, but why?' I whispered.

We crouched there until the boys passed, laughing like pirates, with two wriggling rats impaled on sticks.

'Are you afraid of them?' I asked when the coast was clear.

'No. Yes. No. They don't like me.'

'Why not?'

'They hate me.'

'But why?'

'I don't know.'

'Do you hate them?'

'They hate me because …'

'Because why, Georgie?'

'Because I … because I'm … me.'

It was probably because he was a sissy. Everyone knew that.

Mr Savidge arranged for Georgie to practise for the Feis Ceoil in 'Jodhpur' every day after school. Sometimes when I arrived they'd be having tea or listening to the gramophone. Mr Savidge loved operas and knew the words, even in French or Italian. When his favourite bits came along, he cried without hiding it, darkening a bright silk hankie with his tears.

Then Georgie's name was in the papers: he had won first prize for Pianoforte in the Feis Ceoil. Everyone was delighted; they said it was his ear that he got from his Grandpa and that he'd go far. Mr Savidge paid for a photographer from Ross of Stephen's Green to snap Georgie at the piano (like the Indian Princesses) with himself in it as well. It was a happy snap. Miss Lillian framed it and put it on the table with the pipe collection.

Then one Saturday morning in the middle of a game of 'Relievio', a howl of agony came from Sweeney's house. It was the Auntie Maureen. We all looked at one another. Was someone trying to saw her in half? Or what? Even the dogs knew something was up and ran around in circles, barking. Then the women began rushing into and out of the house, flinching and making faces and the men scurried past it, eyes down, heads into their shoulders, not wanting to know.

At one o'clock when the racket was at its worst, I was going home for my dinner when the door suddenly opened and Mr Sweeney stuck his head out like an old wizened tortoise. I raced over.

'Hello, Mr Sweeney.'

'Eily, the very girl.'

'Is the Auntie Maureen alright?'

'Run down to Cully's for a half an ounce of Mick McQuaid Cut Plug.' He thrust a shilling at me with shaky hands.

'Is she sick or what?'

'Go on now, Eily. Mick McQuaid.'

'But is she—'

'Cut Plug. A half ounce. Hurry.'

The door closed.

Maggie Cully wiped her nose and then the knife in her apron before cutting the tobacco. 'A half-ounce,' she said.

Another drop, like a roundy diamond, appeared by magic on the tip of her nose. It changed into a peardrop and, just as it was about to fall, Georgie rushed into the shop, his face radiant.

'She's dying, Eily!' he shouted. 'Dying.'

'I know. I heard her.'

He looked at Maggie, nearly bursting out of his skin with the happiness. 'My auntie's dying.'

Maggie shrugged and wiped her nose again. 'Is that so?'

'Yeah. Great isn't it? Yippee!'

'Tenpence ha'penny,' said Maggie to me.

On the way up the road we met Father Breen coming down, coat-tails flying, like a big black pirate ship on a breezy day.

'New life, children, new life,' he roared. 'Glory be to God!'

'Yes, Father.'

'Lourdes and Fatima,' he beamed, patting Georgie on the shoulder. 'God bless you all said Tiny Tim.'

'Thank you, Father.'

'Fatima and Lourdes!' He sailed off shouting, followed by the usual band of beady old ladies.

The Auntie Maureen was so protective of her twins that no one was allowed go near them on account of germs. Not that you'd want to; they were awful-looking babies. Fatima was fat and waxy and spent all her time spewing out milk on top of Lourdes, who was small and sickly. Little *dotes*, God bless them, the women said, lying through their teeth. (The Auntie should've heard what they said behind her back.)

One Saturday I found Mr Savidge in a flowery apron icing a nice-looking cake. 'Happy Birthday, Georgie, 15,' he squirted in wobbly pink.

'Lillian's taken him to a matinée at the Gaiety. The Royal Festival Ballet from London. He's never been to a ballet.'

'Has he not?'

'No.'

'Neither have I.'

'Oh!'

'No.'

'Well, perhaps when you're fifteen, if we can still rise to the price of a ticket. One should never neglect beauty, my dear. The finer things of life. Music. Poetry. Art. They exalt the soul. The mind. If you follow me. Lift it up. Up!'

A blob of pink icing flew through air.

'Up where?'

Mr Savidge smiled sadly. 'You could lay the table if you like, Eily. We're using the pink china, so I think perhaps ...'

'The pink cloth?'

'Perfect.'

The ballet, *Swan Lake*, was a great success. Everything about it had delighted Georgie: the music, dancing, the costumes and the scenery. He went on about it so much that I couldn't get a word in edgeways. (To tell the truth I felt a bit jealous.) Miss Lillian agreed that it had been an altogether splendid performance.

Mr Savidge put on a record of 'The Nutcracker Suite', so I took off my shoes and ballet-danced by myself in front of the mirror while Miss Lillian made the tea. Georgie lay among the blue cushions with Gervaise, watching me.

'I see,' said Georgie, when I stopped dancing. 'That's how *not* to do it.'

I didn't think that was very funny.

During the tea-party Georgie announced that he'd like to be a ballet dancer when he grew up. I nearly choked on the cake with the laughing. Miss Lillian hummed and hawed a bit, saying it might be difficult, that boys weren't taught ballet in Ireland where it was not considered manly.

'What about England?' asked Georgie.

'Oh yes. You might do it there.'

I wasn't surprised. I always knew the English were big sissies.

A few days later Mrs Sweeney called me over and handed me an envelope with 'H. Savage. Music teacher' scrawled in purple pencil.

'Give this in to the music-master. And that,' slipping me a hot penny, 'is for yourself, for to buy something with. Be sure to give it into his hand.'

My stomach heaved. Even the letter and the penny smelled of rancid suet.

After reading the letter, Mr Savidge rolled it into a ball and flung it at the wall.

'Philistines!' he shouted.

Gervaise fled.

Miss Lillian frowned. 'Now, Harold. Keep calm.'

'Bloody Philistines!' He marched out of the room.

Miss Lillian picked up the letter and smoothed out the creases. '"Due to pecuniary circumstances, i.e. twins, piano lessons terminated as from today".' She finished it silently. 'Oh no.'

'What? Is someone dead?'

'No. It's just his, Georgie's … they're taking him away from school.'

'Oh!'

'To work in a hardware shop.'

'I love the smell in hardware shops. And no more school. Lucky him.'

Miss Lillian looked out the window to where Mr Savidge stood under the apple tree with Gervaise in his arms. 'Poor chap, so full of promise.'

'What's Philistines?' I asked, but she didn't say anything.

It was a while before I saw Georgie again. I knew he was working and had stopped learning the piano and going up to see the Savidges. Then I gave up the piano too because it was a waste of good money that doesn't grow on trees. But I still went up to 'Jodhpur' sometimes for tea and chats.

One day we were up at the Botanic Gardens looking at trees, which Mr Savidge called specimens. That's a fine specimen, he'd say, pointing with his malacca cane, telling us the particular tree's Latin name, origin and growth habits.

Down by the Japanese bridge we came to a remarkably fine specimen of a *Cedrus Atlantica V. Pendula*, as tall and straight as Nelson's Pillar with thick, dark foliage falling to the ground. I ran in underneath. It was as dark as a cave. And I fell over Mousey Heron and a girl I didn't know (but *not* Queenie Foreman) kissing on the ground.

I scrambled to my feet and ran but Mousey was up like Jack Flash and after me, panting, red-faced, with bits of tree in his hair.

'Hello, Eily,' he said, grabbing me by my arm.

'Hello, Mousey.'

He got between me and the girl.

'It's a hot day, isn't it, Mousey?' I said to be friendly.

'Yeah.'

'Yeah. You look hot. You look roasting.'

He leaned towards me and jerked his head backwards. 'That's eh … that's no one,' he said.

'Is it not?'

'No.'

'Oh.'

'It's eh, it's only my cousin.'

'Oh.'

I looked around him. You could see the girl's vest. She saw me looking and buttoned up her blouse.

'What're you doin' up here anyway?' asked Mousey.

'Looking at specimens.'

'Wha'?'

'With the Savidges. See? There they are.'

Their outlines were just visible through the greeny-black foliage.

'Aw shag it!' said Mousey. He sniffed up a noseful of snot, spat it out, took money from his pocket, chose a threepenny bit and held it out to me. 'Do us a favour,' he winked. 'Don't *say* anything. Twig?'

I looked at the threepenny bit and again at the girl. And then I thought about it.

Mousey shifted impatiently. 'It's only my shaggin' cousin anyway,' he said and took out a sixpence.

'Thanks, Mousey.'

Groups of people lazed along the banks of the Tolka. Willy-wag-tails swooped, skittering across the top of the water, catching flies, and tall willows dipped as if for a drink, their leaves silvering in the sun.

'Isn't that young Georgie?' asked Miss Lillian, looking towards a fellow in long trousers who was reading under a rhododendron bush.

'Yeah, look at him. He has longers on,' I said, laughing.

As if he knew he was being talked about, Georgie looked up and then, deliberately, away.

'Hey! What's up with you?'

Miss Lillian took my arm. 'I think he'd rather be alone.'

Mr Savidge, looking hurt, went home to listen to a little Gigli before tea.

Miss Lillian and I walked to a shady place where squirrels raced up and down tall trees.

'Georgie hasn't been to see us since he started work,' said Miss Lillian.

'I know.'

'I wonder how he's getting on.'

'Do you?'

'Yes. I'd like to know. We miss him. And I feel sorry for him somehow. He's such a lonely young fellow.'

'Well it's his own fault. He never pals around with anyone, and the big boys hate him, they call him names, girls' names, Georgina.'

Miss Lillian closed her eyes and shook her head.

The squirrels were having great fun, throwing nuts and pine-cones and bits of tree-bark at each other.

'They called my brother names too,' Miss Lillian said, smoothing the fingers of her cream cotton gloves. 'At boarding-school in

England. It made his life one long misery.'

'Yeah but my Ma says that sticks and stones can break your bones but names can never hurt you.'

'Indeed. Names can't break your bones. But they can break your heart, Eily. And that's worse.' She sighed. 'I wonder what'll become of Georgie. He's a vulnerable boy.'

'And he thinks he's great too just because he has longers on.'

Then, one lucky Saturday, at *Kiss of Death* I found a half-crown down the side of the seat. As soon as the last note of the national anthem finished, I raced over to the Broadway-Ritz to spend it on a sitting-down ice-cream. It was packed with the usual Saturday mob; they spilled out of the booths, talking, laughing and enjoying themselves. Mousey Heron and the big boys were at the juke-box, jostling and pucking each other the way they do. Bob Hope was singing 'Buttons and Bows'.

Georgie was sitting in the very last booth all by himself.

'Hello, Georgie.'

He gave me a dirty look. But I slid in along the seat opposite him. 'At the flicks, were you? Great, wasn't it, the big one? I love Richard Widmark, do you?'

He looked around as if trying to escape. But there was nowhere else to sit.

'I found this half-crown down the side of the seat. Lucky, wasn't it? I always look, but I never found anything before, only hairpins and orange peel and once a miraculous medal on a pin.'

Queenie Foreman, the waitress, perched one curvy hip on the edge of our table and gazed through black-beaded lashes at a small soldier who stood at the bus stop picking his nose.

'Wattle yiz have?' she asked in a bored voice, taking a pencil from the pocket of her tight pink uniform.

'A large strawberry sundae with whipped cream please, Queenie,' I said.

She made a mark in her notebook, turned and thrust her big chest at Georgie.

'The same for me,' he said hurriedly, backing away.

Queenie arched a thinly pencilled eyebrow, tossed her yellow hair and sashayed up to the counter on her three-inch red heels.

'Ay, Marco, two large straws, whipped!' she yelled, leaning on the counter.

'She's gorgeous, isn't she?' I said. 'Like Jane Russell in *The Paleface*, only different colour hair.'

'Jesus Christ,' muttered Georgie in a deep, man's voice.

'Do you like going to work? How do you like it?'

'I hate it. I loathe it.'

'I bet it's better than school though.'

'It isn't.'

'Getting pay is better though.'

'No it's not.'

'But—'

'Do you not understand English? I hate it.'

'Keep your hair on. I only asked.'

'Do you know what I do all day?' He looked at me as if it was all my fault.

'What?'

'I count screws. Screws. Bloody screws. Can you imagine that? And nuts.'

'So what?'

'Here yiz are,' interrupted Queenie. 'Two large straws.'

We had taken about three spoonfuls of the delicious dreamy ice-cream when a hand slammed down on our table.

'Well, lookee who's here.' It was Mousey Heron, grinning down like a hyena. He sat in beside Georgie, squashing him up against the wall. 'Come on, men, siddown, siddown. In here. With Georgie-Porgy. Room for one and all.'

There wasn't, but Fatrat, Breadhorse and the others did as they were told, piling into the booth, pushing me against the wall too. I pushed back.

Mousey put one arm around Georgie's shoulder. 'That right, Georgina? Bucketsa room.'

He laughed. The boys laughed. Georgie's face paled. Then Mousey took Georgie's spoon and coolly helped himself to a huge mouthful of his ice-cream. Smacking his hairy lips, he slid the dish along the table. 'Help yourselves, men. Georgie'd like you to have a bit of his, wouldn't you, Georgie dear?' Pushing his face into Georgie's.

The boys brayed like donkeys. Georgie's head was against the wall. His face was chalk-white. Breadhorse Butler started to wolf his ice-cream.

'That's not fair,' I said in a loud voice. 'It's not your ice-cream. Georgie paid for it.'

There was a small silence. They all looked at me in surprise.

'Well, isn't that nice?' jeered Mousey. 'Georgie has a *fwend*. A little girl-fwend. Now tell us, Georgie, cos we'd all like to know, what do you *do* with her?'

The boys exploded with laughter.

Mousey grabbed Georgie's hand and squeezed it, his knuckles going white with the effort. 'You like us better though,' he said softly. 'Don't you, Georgie?'

Georgie looked as if he was going to cry. I had to do something.

'Yeah, well,' I shouted above the din, looking straight at Mousey. 'Some of us better remember that we have *cousins*!'

Mousey's mouth dropped open.

Queenie descended as if on cue. 'Yizzle all hafta quit that shoutin' or yizzle be thrun out.'

'It's all his fault, Queenie.' I pointed at Mousey, who was staring at me like a hypnotized ferret. 'He took Georgie's ice-cream and won't leave us alone. He's nothing but a big bully so he is and if I wasn't a girl I'd do him in.'

Queenie inflated herself like a pink balloon and gave Mousey a look of melting passion. 'Ah, Jayziss, sweetie, wudja ever lay off.'

Mousey gave the sign, so they all sloped off and me and Georgie finished our ice-creams in peace.

On the way home there was a bit of excitement outside the church where a number nine bus had crashed into a milkman's horse which was dying in the middle of the road. People milled around to see.

'Trigger, oh Trigger,' moaned the milkman, sitting on the kerb, crying into his cap. 'My old pal.'

The driver climbed out of the bus, took off his cap and sat down beside the milkman. Father Breen dashed out of the presbytery wearing a hairnet and a worn pair of wine velvet slippers.

'Air, give him air, can't you! Air,' he shouted, spreading his long arms to push back the crowd.

'It's only a bloody horse,' said a voice.

'Horse or not, it's a life,' retorted Father Breen, whipping out his Rosary beads. 'In the name of the Father …'

We all knelt down. In the middle of the Agony in the Garden, the horse tried to get up, then fell down and died. I was nearly crying.

'I say,' said a well-dressed voice from the bus. 'I'm frightfully sorry but—'

'Oh lah-di-dah,' someone shouted.

'I'm due in Donnybrook at half-past six. Do you think … is there any possibility …?'

The horse was dragged to the side of the road. The bus took off. Men put their hats back on. Father Breen threw a blanket over the horse and brought the milkman into the presbytery for a cup of tea. Beggars started begging. People drifted off, the men explaining to the women precisely how it had happened.

'He'll probably go to the knacker's now,' said Georgie as we walked home together.

'What's the knacker's?'

'The knacker's yard. O'Keeffe's the knacker. Where they burn horses for glue.'

'They do not.'

'They do so.'

'Liar liar pants on fire hanging out of a telegraph wire.'

'I'm not a liar. You know that smell every Thursday?'

'That stink?'

'Yeah.'

'It's awful.'

'Well, that stink's the knacker's yard, but you needn't believe me if you don't want to.'

'Glue?'

'Yeah.'

We walked along. Georgie dribbled an empty tin can along the pavement.

'Georgie.'

'What?'

'Why don't you go up to see the Savidges any more?'

He kicked the tin away. 'Misfit,' he muttered.

'Miss Lillian was wondering.'

'Let her. I don't care.'

'Don't care was made care.'

'Oh, shut up you and leave me alone.'

'You know what you are, Georgie Sweeney?'

'Yes. I know what I am.' His eyes were bright with tears. 'I'm nothing but a sissy. A big sissy. The biggest sissy of them all.'

He ran into his house.

My Ma pounced on me as soon as I was in the door. 'And where were you till now, Miss?'

'The pictures, a bus ran over a horse and—'

'Until now?'

'No, I had a sitting-down ice-cream in the Broadway-Ritz with Georgie and—'

'Georgie *Sweeney?*'

'Yes and on the way home a bus—'

'What were you doing with him?'

'Nothing. But a horse got—'

'What was he saying to you? What did he *want* with you?'

'Nothing. He told me about the knacker's.'

'The *what?*'

'The knacker's. Where the smell on a Thursday comes from.'

'Jesus, Mary and Joseph!' She marched off to the kitchen and came back with a plate on which there were two burnt sausages, half a tomato and a piece of white pudding. 'Here,' plonking it down in front of me. 'Eat that. It's probably stone cold by now and dry as a bone but that's no one's fault but your own and keep away from that misfit Georgie Sweeney in future.'

'What's a misfit?'

'Eat your sausage.'

★

On New Year's Day we met the Auntie Maureen out wheeling the twins, who were like white rats in their rabbit-fur bonnets. Fatima was fatter and oilier than before, and Lourdes skinnier. They smelled of suet.

The Auntie Maureen gave Mammy a Craven A, removed a wadge of suet from her mouth and threw it into the snow.

'I suppose you heard the news,' she said.

'What news was that?' said Mammy.

'The young fella.'

'No. What about him?'

'Run off with himself.'

'What? He didn't! Georgie? When?'

'Without as much as a by-your-leave. A bit of a note for the Da and that was it. After all I done for him, washin', scrubbin', feedin' him and gettin' the job and all, and that's the thanks I get.'

'That's terrible. And where's he gone?' asked Mammy, with a face as if she cared.

'I understand it's across the water.'

'To England?'

'Aye. To join the Navy. Best place for him, the sea. It'll make a man of him. Always a bit of a misfit if you ask me.'

I went up to 'Jodhpur' with the news. Miss Lillian, with Gervaise on her lap, just kept looking into the fire as if she was seeing pictures there.

'They said he's a misfit,' I said, as if that might explain it.

Mr Savidge poured out more tea. 'The world is full of misfits, Eily. But it's a big world. There should be room for all of us.'

We listened to a recording of Count John McCormack singing 'The Last Rose of Summer'. Then I went home.

A CLOSE SHAVE
WITH THE DEVIL

The devil was going around again and everyone knew because it was in the papers. An usherette in The Metropole saw him at *An Apartment for Peggie*, eating oranges in a brown trilby; two women in Clery's Bargain Basement came upon him fingering cups in a highly suspicious manner; and the *Evening Mail* said pretty draper's assistant, Lily Shine, nineteen, from Cabra West, was dancing with a fellow in a brown suit in the Ballerina Ballroom when she felt something funny, looked down, and fainted.

It was The Cloven Foot!

Father Breen knew too and warned us from the pulpit at the Friday night Sodality meeting.

'Beware, my children.' His voice boomed down into our heads and up into the high shadows of the vaulted ceiling. He leaned forward, long arms outstretched, as though to embrace and protect us all. 'Many faces he has, the devil. Many names. Beelzebub. And many disguises. And you must learn to recognise them. To be on your guard. Ever vigilant. Swords at the ready. To be prepared to fight, yea, even unto death itself, against the snares he has laid to destroy you. To trap and destroy you. To putrify your purity. Your holy purity. That pearl beyond price. That greatest gift of God most High. Recognise and … *destroy*!' Smashing his hand down, raising dust, making us jump. 'Smite him with all his works and pomps. Crush him as our Holy Virgin Mother crushed him with her Blessed Heel. And cast him into eternal flames forever. In the name of the Father, Son and Holy Ghost Amen.'

He disappeared. The organ swelled. We stood to sing the hymn:

Jesus Lord I ask for Mercy.
Let me not implore in vain.
All my sins I now detest them.
Never will I sin again.
By my sins I have deserved
Death and endless misery,
Hell, with all its pains and torments,
And for all eternity.

'What's holy purity anyway?' I asked Gracie Fox on the way home.

'I don't know, but it's awful cos you go straight to hell if you haven't got it.'

'I know that but—'

A man in a dirty raincoat stepped out from the shadows, took a hold of my sleeve.

'Hey, young one.'

'What?'

'Do your Ma and Da sleep in the same b-b-b-b-b-b-b-'

'Bed. Yeah, why? Do yours not?'

He looked surprised, then shuffled off without saying anything else.

'Who's he when he's at home and what's he want?' asked Gracie when I caught up with her.

'I dunno. Nothing. He has an awful stammer.'

'The thing about holy purity is, you're born with it,' Gracie explained. 'Everybody has it when they're young. Even you.'

'Have I?'

'Yeah.'

'But what is it?'

'And you have to say three Hail Marys every night or else the devil gets it and you're cast into internal flames forever.'

I asked Father Breen at confession next morning. He buried his nose in a huge hankie and blew like a foghorn.

'It's God's greatest gift, Eily. A pearl beyond price.'

'Yes, Father, but what *is* it?'

'Three Hail Marys every night and Our Holy Mother will protect you.' He yawned. 'Any more out there?'

'No, Father, I'm the last.'

'Ah, *Deo gratias*! Good child. Run along so. God bless you.'

'But—'

'Pray for me.' He turned off his light and left me in the dark.

The church was like heaven for the Sodality Mass on Sunday morning, with the candles, silk-fringed banners, starched altar-cloths and the choir singing sweetly as seraphim. Four shiny altar-boys with watered-down hair attended Father Breen, who whirled about like God the Father in his gold and silver chasuble.

Pew by pew we queued up to receive Holy Communion, boys on one side, girls on the other, a churchful of spotless children in our Sunday best. I knelt at the altar-rail with the cool linen clasped against my throat. 'Dear Jesus my Lord my God my All, forgive me my sins, let Mammy and Daddy come home safely always and let me keep my holy purity till death do us part, I love you.' The altar-boy pressed the paten beneath my chin. 'Corpus Christi,' muttered Father Breen, placing the Host on my tongue. I walked back to my pew with downcast eyes, trying to swallow it before it stuck like glue to the roof of my mouth because it was a sin (only venial, but still) to poke at it with your tongue. But I was lucky that morning; it slid down like a Woolworth's ice-cream.

I felt so holy and full of sanctifying grace that when Mass was over I ran straight across the road without looking, hoping a bus would knock me down and up into the heavenly Kingdom that

Jesus had prepared for the Blessed of His Father. But it didn't, so I ran home with the Sunday-morning smell of crisping rashers curling around the corner to meet me.

After breakfast, I helped Hippo-Joe, the groundsman, to pin up notices for the dance:

BLARNEY PARK ANNUAL MARQUEE DANCE
To the Music of
BOB MCGARRIGLE AND HIS BOBCATS

Spots	Raffles	Refreshments
Dress Informal	Dancing 9 to 1	Admission 5/

'Will you be going, Hippo-Joe?'

'Naw.'

His face flushed. Hippo-Joe was a huge, shy man who kept himself to himself. My Ma thought he was a bit peculiar, but she thought that about a lot of people. When we finished the notices, I stood at the door of Hippo-Joe's shed watching him mix white powder from a tin marked with a red skull-and-crossbones.

'Is that poison?'

'Yep. Deadly.'

'What for?'

'Rats. What d'you think?' His eyes were as soft and brown as turf. He nodded towards the meadow of long waving grass at the top of the courts. 'Come up with me and I'll show you.'

'Ah no. My dinner'll be ready.'

The thought of rats made me shiver.

On Wednesday afternoon, because Mammy had a headache, I was sent into Cavendishes in Grafton Street to pay the five shillings HP off the sideboard. After I had paid it, I stood looking into Fuller's window with the water sloshing around my mouth.

'Well, Glory be to God, but aren't they lovely buns and cakes?' said a holy voice with a country accent.

I looked up. It was a tall priest.

'Yes, Father.'

'They'd cost the earth, I suppose?'

'I suppose so, Father.'

'Indeed they would, God knows, and tell me, little one, what is it your name is?'

'Eily Doolin, Father.'

'Oh, a lovely name, God bless it. A good saint's name.' He smiled. 'Now tell me, Eily alannah, are you all by yourself in town today?'

'Yes, Father. Mammy has a headache so—'

'A headache? Oh, poor soul. There's nothing worse. Did she ever try the blessed Lourdes water, I wonder?'

'I don't know, Father.'

'Oh, she should, she should, tis a miracle cure and do you know what I'm going to tell you, Eily?'

'No, Father.'

'Tis your Mammy's lucky day because I have some that was given into these hands last week by His Holiness the Pope.'

'The Pope?'

'God bless him. In the panting heart of Rome itself. Plagued with the headaches he is, our great and good Pontiff, but swears by the blessed Lourdes water. So you come along with me now, I live up just up here, and I'll give you the blessed water for your poor Mammy, God love her.'

He bent to take my hand and I got a whiff of what you get when you lift some scrunchy seaweed and it's all soft and rotting underneath.

We turned into South King Street and were hurrying past the Gaiety Theatre when suddenly a green umbrella came flying over our heads.

'Stop! Stop him!' shouted a fat woman, running up behind us waving a crucifix.

'Fuck it,' shouted the priest. He hared off up the road, around by Mercer's Hospital, out of sight.

The woman eased herself down, puffing and panting, onto the step of the theatre, then fixed me with a look. 'Are you alright?'

'Yes, thanks. Grand.'

'Praise be to God.'

She took off her hat and fanned herself with it. Beads of sweat glistened on her little blonde moustache. 'That bowsy has my heart scalded,' she said, raising her voice. 'Scalded!'

A skinny doorman in a too-big uniform poked his head out the door. 'What's up, Missis?'

'Apart from the sky, nothing that a glassa water wouldn't fix, if it's all the same to you thanks.'

He nodded, causing his peaked cap to slip over one eye. 'Never let it be said,' he said and disappeared.

I picked up the woman's umbrella, which had got a bit buckled, and gave it to her. She thanked me, asked me my name. I told her.

'Well, Eily Doolin and did your Mammy never tell you not to be talking to strangers and you down-town all by yourself?'

'Yes.'

'Well? And what had you talking to that fella so?'

'But he's not a stranger. He's a priest.'

'Priest? Hah! Priest me eye! That fella's no more a priest nor I am.'

'Is he not?'

'Divil the bit.'

'He looks like a priest.'

'A ruse, child.'

'And he sounds like a priest.'

'A right blaggard that's all he is!'

'And he said the Pope gave him Lourdes water.'

'Wudja listen to me? Wudja ever listen? Amn't I after tellin' you? It's a ruse. The whole thing. A disguise to trap you. To get you to go with him.'

'Go where?'

The doorman returned with a huge glass of water which the woman drank all in the one go.

'By gob but you've a powerful swally,' said he, waggling in admiration.

The woman nodded, drying her chin with her hat. 'Yes, thanks be to God.' She kissed her crucifix, wrapped it in red flannel that smelled of Sloan's liniment and placed it in her shopping-bag. 'I never go anywhere without it these days,' she said to the doorman. 'Things being the way they are.'

He agreed. 'Oh, a compulsory item nowadays alright, the crucifix. A compulsory item.'

He straightened out her umbrella and helped to haul her to her feet. She told him he was one of Nature's gentlemen, then took my hand and walked me to the bus stop, saying she wouldn't be easy in her mind until I was safely on the bus.

'Because you know what you've just had, Eily Doolin?'

'No. What?'

'A close shave. With the devil himself. Beelzebub. A very close shave.'

It all came back in a rush: the usherette in The Metropole, the fingered cups and Lily Shine in a faint in the Ballerina Ballroom. Father Breen's words rang in my head: many faces and disguises had the devil, to trap, destroy and putrify.

'Be careful, Eily,' the woman warned in a low voice. 'You may not be so lucky the next time.'

The devil was after me!

As the bus passed the Rotunda Hospital, a man in a brown hat unlocking his bicycle from the railings looked up at me and sneered; in Dorset Street another, disguised as a postman, spat and gave me a look; going over Cross Guns Bridge a red-eyed coalman stood up in his cart waving his whip as if to say, 'I'll get you, Eily Doolin. I'll get you yet.'

I started to say a Rosary every night on my fingers to the picture of Our Lady hanging over my bed. It was one with the eyes that follow you as long as you're pure and without sin. When, last thing at night, her blue eyes looked lovingly down into mine, I knew I was protected and safe from all harm. (I always checked under the bed too, just in case, but there was never anything there, except rolling footballs of fluff, like candyfloss at a carnival.)

On the Saturday afternoon three of us with leather soles were allowed into the marquee to make the floor good and slippy for the dance that night. It was beautiful: gay and festive with balloons, streamers, bunting and, right in the centre, a shimmering crystal ball. Up on the bandstand a man tested the microphone, 'Baa-baa black sheep have you any wool? Yes sir, yes sir, three bags full.' Another practised 'Where or When?' on a clarinet. At the entrance, behind a trestle-table, big fellows discussed Stan Kenton with serious faces while stacking crates of Cantrell & Cochrane Lemonade, Raspberry and American Cream Soda.

Later, some tennis-playing girls moseyed in, highstepping, smoothskinned, cool in white Aertex. 'H'mm, not bad,' they murmured, testing the floor like creamy long-legged cats. 'Not bad at all.' Glancing slyly along their shoulders, until the fellows ran and took them in their arms, whirling them around the floor like Fred Astaire and Ginger.

It must be great to be grown up, I thought, as they drifted dreamily through a haze of flying dustmotes. With lipstick, powder, slim brown legs, staying up late and knowing everything.

Des-the-Wolf came along, gave us a bottle of Raspberry for doing good work on the floor.

Then everyone hurried home for their tea.

I went into the Ladies Cloakroom in the pavilion to get my

cardigan and when I came out Hippo-Joe was standing in the corner looking at the wall which was covered with photographs of prize-winners.

'Who's that up there, Eily?' he asked, squinting up at a particular photo. 'Can you make it out?'

'The marquee's smashing, isn't it?' I said.

He nodded, but kept peering up at the photograph.

'I'd go to the dance if I was you. The floor's lovely and slippy now and there's great spots and raffles and all.'

He lifted me up onto the long wooden bench that went all around the pavilion, and stood behind me. 'Who's that? Can you see?'

'Yeah. It's Mister Gough with the cup last year. "P.J. Gough. Men's Singles. Nineteen-forty-eight." I better go now cos my tea'll be ready.'

He held on to my legs. 'And who's that?' he asked quickly.

'That?'

His hands started sliding up and down.

'That's the German, Frank N. Stein.'

He leaned his weight into me, squeezing my legs, his hands moving further up under my frock. I began to be afraid. 'There's Gorgeous Gussie Moran!' he said in a strange voice. 'What d'you think of her?'

Feeling suddenly trapped and terrified, I stared into a mouthful of gleaming white teeth. 'A bit like a horse,' I said in a whisper.

'Yes, she's nice, isn't she nice? Yes. But not as nice as you.'

I tried to pull away but then he had me. His fingers. I froze. Staring into the screaming smile of Gorgeous Gussie Moran. And all the while his voice. 'Oh nice yes nice, but not as you, nor half as nice, my little, aren't you yes, my own little lovely angel.' Taking my hand then, putting it down onto something soft and clammy, closing my fingers around it, whispering. 'Mine now you are, all mine, my little angel.'

I woke up in the middle of the night, sore, and I knew. That was holy purity and mine was gone. He had taken it. My pearl of great price. The devil in disguise had trapped and destroyed. Putrified me. I was now his. His angel. Damned for all eternity. On Judgment Day, God the Father would turn and curse me from a height with the terrible words: 'Depart from me, ye cursèd, into the everlasting flames which were prepared for the Devil and his angels.'

I switched on the light. Our Lady wouldn't look at me. I ran from here to there and back, but no matter where I was, her eyes were somewhere else. I stood on the bed and looked right into her face. She looked up to heaven, beseeching her only begotten Son to get her out of the company of this vile and tainted sinner.

I tried a perfect act of contrition but forgot the words. Jeering voices rang in my ears:

> *Out of hell there's no redemption.*
> *When you go there you get a pension.*
> *Threepence a week, working hard.*
> *Chasing the Devil around the yard.*

But I wasn't there yet.

At ten o'clock Mass the next morning, at the Consecration, the very moment when the priest changed the bread and wine into the Body and Blood of Our Lord Jesus Christ, the idea leaped into my head. It had to do with the skull-and-crossbones tin and the fresh jam-tarts that Mammy made every Sunday morning.

It was a heavy, sleepy kind of a day. Apart from two boys playing tennis over in the children's section, the club was empty. I lay down near the marquee waiting, wondering if he'd appear, praying he would.

Everything was ready. I had my two jam-tarts.

The smell of Sunday dinners woke me up: roast beef, bacon and cabbage, thyme-and-onion-stuffed chicken. And suddenly there he was, in the lane, talking to Gracie Fox's little sister, Annie.

I stood up slowly to let him see me, then turned around and lay back down, stretching myself out, my hands folded behind my head.

The next minute he was standing over me, looking down, rattling money in his trouser pockets.

I just lay there saying nothing.

He looked around. Lit a cigarette. Plucked a shred of tobacco from his lower lip. Rubbed it into the lapel of his suit which was the same turf-brown as his eyes.

'Didja go to the dance?' I asked.

His thick, black eyebrows drew together. 'Naw.'

I turned over onto my stomach. A black ant dragged a dead fly backwards towards a tiny hole in the ground. When it got there, the ant went around to the other side of the fly and began to push it down into the hole. The fly was too big to go easily but the ant kept pushing, poking and squashing it in.

'Come on into the tent,' the devil said softly, his red lips barely moving. 'Come on.'

My heart beat like a drum. 'Have a jam-tart.'

'*What?*'

I sat up and unwrapped one. 'A jam-tart. They're lovely. My Ma makes them. Here.'

'I don't like jam.'

'Ah go on.' I smiled. 'And then I'll go in.'

He grabbed, shoved it into his mouth and ate it quickly. 'Come on.'

I stood up, then handed him the second one. 'It'll only go stale.'

He wolfed it down.

You'd think a horde of savages had invaded the marquee: it stank; everything was destroyed; benches overturned, the bunting torn down, balloons burst; stout bottles dribbled like drunkards on the floor, with cigarette butts, used matches, vomit pools, torn raffle tickets.

And yesterday—was it only yesterday? When everything was beautiful, bright and clean, and the dancers danced in the golden light.

A yellow balloon floated down from nowhere. I caught and cradled it in my arms.

Yesterday was dead and gone. Today was different. I knew that nothing would ever be the same.

He lay sprawled out on the trestle-table. 'Come here,' he whispered. 'Come and talk to me.'

I took a small step towards him, praying with all my might that it would happen. But afraid, afraid. Another slow step closer. Mouth dry with terror. Almost crying. Then, in the middle of the third step, he groaned and sat up, grabbing his stomach.

'Christ,' he roared. 'Jesus!' He fell back, legs up to his belly, whimpering like a dog. The pain was so fierce, I nearly felt sorry. Then remembered. His face was waxy, shiny with sweat. Moaning, he tumbled off the table down into the dirt. 'Jesus, help me.'

I sat on the table.

He rolled himself over onto his stomach and tried to claw his way out, splintering the floor with his dirty brown nails. Then, gulping air, he threw his head back. Sudsy foam bubbled from his mouth. He collapsed, lay still. Just when I thought he was finished, he lifted his head and looked up with terrible blood-filled eyes.

'Help me,' he begged, stretching out his hand. 'Help.'

I stood on the hand. With all my weight I crushed that hand as hard as I could, like Our Holy Virgin Mother did when he was the Serpent. 'You're going to die,' I told him. 'This time. For once and for all.'

I made a pile with papers and rubbish, took the matches from his pocket and put a light to it. In no time at all flames licked and crackled around him like a forest fire.

Redemption, I knew it. I could feel it, could hear the heavens sing in praise of me.

I looked back through the smoke. 'Depart from me, ye cursèd, into everlasting flames which were prepared for you and your angels,' I shouted.

Then I went home for my dinner.

On the way down the lane a sudden breeze lifted the yellow balloon from my arms. I ran, leaping after it. But it was no good. Off it went, drifting higher and higher, over the rooftops, then into the clouds, a small yellow sun, gone forever.